MASQUERADE FOR MURDER
A MIKE HAMMER NOVEL

MORE MIKE HAMMER
FROM TITAN BOOKS

MASQUERADE FOR MURDER

A MIKE HAMMER NOVEL

MICKEY SPILLANE

and

MAX ALLAN COLLINS

TITANBOOKS

Masquerade for Murder: A Mike Hammer Novel
Print edition ISBN: 9781785655562
E-book edition ISBN: 9781785655579

Published by Titan Books
A division of Titan Publishing Group Ltd
144 Southwark St, London SE1 0UP

First edition: March 2020

1 3 5 7 9 10 8 6 4 2

A CIP catalogue record for this title is available from the British Library.

Printed and bound in the United States.

What did you think of this book? We love to hear from our readers.
Please email us at readerfeedback@titanemail.com or write to us at
Reader Feedback at the above address.

To receive advance information, news, competitions, and exclusive
Titan offers online, please sign up for the Titan newsletter on our website:
www.titanbooks.com

FOR GARY SANDY –

who brought Mike alive on stage

CO-AUTHOR'S NOTE

Shortly before his death in 2006, Mickey Spillane told his wife Jane, "When I'm gone, there's going to be a treasure hunt around here. Take everything you find and give it to Max—he'll know what to do."

Working under the death sentence of pancreatic cancer, Mickey had already called me to ask if I would complete his final Mike Hammer novel for him, if that became necessary, which it did—the greatest, if most bittersweet, honor of my career.

Half a dozen substantial Hammer manuscripts of 100 pages or more were found in the "treasure hunt," conducted by Jane, my wife Barb and me. These five lost Hammer novels spanned Mickey's career, from the late '40s through the mid-'60s and on up to (and including) *The Goliath Bone*, which he was working on at the time of his passing.

The six substantial manuscripts—often with notes, sometimes with roughed-out endings—were the first order of business; these have all been completed. A number of shorter but significant Hammer manuscripts—again, sometimes with notes and rough endings—were also worthy of completion, including the writer's first attempt at a Hammer yarn (*Killing Town*, 2018). Some less substantial fragments became short stories, eight of which have been collected in *A Long Time Dead*, published by Mysterious Press.

This time—as was the case with the previous Hammer novel, *Murder, My Love* (2019)—I am working chiefly from a synopsis, with only a few tasty morsels of Spillane prose to interweave. As usual, I have done my best to determine when Mickey wrote the material, so that I might set the novel in continuity, to give the book its rightful place in the canon.

The nature of the plot synopsis suggests *Masquerade for Murder* may have been designed for one of actor Stacy Keach's *Mike Hammer* telefilms or episodes of the TV series that ended in 1989 (revived in 1997). I know that Mickey developed several ideas for TV producer Jay Bernstein, and in fact his novel *The Killing Man* (1989) began that way, until Mickey decided to go the prose route ("It was too good to waste on television," he told me). Mickey also devised the ending of the otherwise abysmal Bernstein-produced, non-Keach Hammer telefilm, *Come Die with Me* (1994), a production Spillane disavowed.

This synopsis would appear to have been developed either before or after *The Killing Man*, putting its action in the late '80s. I am placing it in the continuity right after that 1989 novel (the text of which places the action in 1988). This presents a Mike Hammer in his late fifties, somewhat younger than the calendar would have him, a mathematical improbability that did not bother Mickey Spillane one bit.

You shouldn't let it bother you, either.

Max Allan Collins
September 2019

CHAPTER ONE

It wasn't New York any more, not the old New York. Over on the Main Stem, the lights still blazed as bright as ever and the people were just as many, but that was Tourist Town. Action Street. The Big Beanery.

And when you stood on the corner of Second and 44th, on a chill November night promising winter, and watched five lanes of taxis cruise by heading south in time with the signals, you knew you had kissed off the old New York a long time ago. The Els were down, the cobwebs gone, and even the slop chutes had their faces lifted. The Blue Ribbon restaurant was a memory, fading into history with Broadway pen pushers like Walter Winchell, Earl Wilson and Hy Gardner, whose newspapers were as dead as they were. The hole-in-the-wall joints were done-over and intimate now, the prices high and the lighting low, where the rich married slobs could slip off with some poor sexy broad without causing too much of a stir. Even the junk shops catered to class. Now they had hand-carved ANTIQUES signs over the doors, and brand-new price tags on the same old worthless rummage.

Across the street from where the hackie dropped me, one place was still open and unchanged—PETE'S CHOPHOUSE, said the neon lettering above dark-tinted windows that glowed with electric beer signs like fireflies in the night. I was meeting Captain Pat Chambers of Homicide, my oldest friend in the world, going back all the way to the army and the kind of war nobody protested. One of his best officers, Lt. Casey Shannon—"the Wall Street Cop," the *News* called him—was retiring soon, and this was his send-off.

Diminutive Pete himself met me just inside—he was his own maitre d', a small jet-black-haired man in his sixties (only his hairdresser knew for sure) wearing a shiny tuxedo and a thick mustache and a puffy face that bore a smile like a duty, but one he didn't mind. The place was smoky and dark, mirrored walls working to make the joint bigger—one of those male bastions where women were welcome, as long as they came accompanied. Like me, Pete's was a relic—a supper club clinging desperately to the past.

"Mike!" Pete said, the smile turning real. "Or is it Mr. Hammer now that you're respectable?"

I grinned at him. "I just killed somebody important for a change."

I took off my porkpie fedora and Pete helped me out of the trenchcoat and took the hat and handed the works over to the blonde at her window; she was maybe twenty-five but in that low-cut sparkly thing, she looked like fifty-five—1955, that is, and that was fine by me.

"One of these serial killers you read about, huh?" Pete burbled. "Hidin' in plain sight, in a government job yet! And you flush him out. You got a lotta play in the papers, Mr. Hammer, Mike—like the old days! Your girl Velda, she's okay? Bastard put her in the hospital, they say."

"She's great. That was months ago, Pete. Old news."

I patted his shoulder and slipped away—I wasn't here to talk to an aging restauranteur about my latest fifteen minutes of infamy.

The hostess, a stunning redhead in a green evening dress with matching emerald eyes, intercepted me. Though I hadn't been to Pete's for a while, I was enough of a regular to know that her first name was Sheila, though by now we were too well-acquainted for me to ask what her last name was.

She was ten curvy pounds the right side of plump and had cherry-red lipsticked lips with a bruised Bardot look that made her smile seem knowing and sly without even trying. Her arm slipped into the crook of mine as she slow-walked me, winding around tables, pausing for bus boys and wait staff.

"Alone tonight, Mike?" She was flirty in that way that you knew would never amount to anything.

"Velda doesn't like this place."

Lovely raven-haired Velda was officially my secretary but unofficially my partner in a bunch of ways, with her own P.I. license and a .32 automatic in her purse and my heart tucked under her arm.

The Bardot lips twitched with amusement. "Food not to Velda's taste?"

"Food very much to her taste. That's why she doesn't like it."

Sheila gave me a kiss of a smile. "Watching her figure?"

"Her and me and every other right-minded man in town. Are you okay, kid?"

"Super. Why?"

"I got X-ray vision. Me and Clark Kent. I can see right through that make-up."

Her left eye was a little swollen and expertly dabbed with flesh-colored cosmetic.

She frowned just a tad. "Is it that obvious, Mike?"

"Could be I'm a detective. What's his name? I might have something for him."

She brought us to a stop and her smile turned into a tragic thing that wouldn't fool anybody. "No, Mike. Please don't. Please stay out of it. I'm breaking it off. I promise. I swear."

I touched her cheek, lightly. "You have any trouble shaking loose, kid, you know where to find me. And it won't cost you a penny. I enjoy spending time with men who think beating up women is fun."

She swallowed, nodded, then delivered me to my destination and slipped back to her post.

Pat hadn't lined up a backroom or anything, just a big corner booth filled with rumpled men in rumpled suits. I shook hands with everybody, then squeezed in next to Pat, who was my age, blond with gray-blue eyes, a trimly muscular build, and a methodical mind.

"We decided," Pat said, "not to wait for you before we started drinking."

"Good call," I said.

There were seven of us, including but not limited to burly, balding Shannon himself; Chris Peters, his slim young current partner on the PD; and Ben Higgins, an already retired skin-and-bones copper who'd been the sidekick before that.

I'd barely settled when a waitress in a white dress shirt and black skirt delivered me a Canadian Club and ginger. Like I said, I was something of a regular at Pete's. My preferences were known.

We talked old times. I won't bore you with it, but Peters loved hearing everything, particularly the tales that showed how dogged and tough Shannon could be, but also the ones that made this older mentor of his seem human, like when the Wall Street Cop was on the receiving end of his former partner Ben Higgins's practical jokes.

"Hell," Higgins was saying, "I didn't even *know* you could melt Ex-Lax down and make a decent hot fudge sundae out of it. Turns out you can!"

Over everybody else's laughter, a smirking Shannon said, "It made hot fudge all right, let me tell you."

Several rounds of drinks went by before we finally ordered. Everybody got the house specialty—bone-in rib-eyes—and the waitress was still getting the particulars, salad dressing, veggies, potato and so on, when a tall, broad-shouldered guy of maybe thirty-five came in, leading two men a decade or so older who seemed vaguely servile yet bore a distinguished quality the younger man somehow lacked.

They were peeling out of their Burberry cashmere trenches, the older men revealing Brooks Brothers suits each worth a week of my rent at the Hackard Building. Shannon—sitting next to Pat—leaned over and said to both of us, "What the hell are *they* doing in a joint like this?"

Shannon looked something like the old movie actor Pat O'Brien at a similar age, but less hair, wisps of white only. Like that old-time actor, he had a hint of Ireland in his voice—not from once having lived there, but growing up in a home where the parents had, and the brogue had been catching.

That other Pat said, "Don't let Pete hear you calling his white-tablecloth joint a joint, pal."

Shannon raised a single hand of surrender. "No, it's not that. It's just…that Colby kid is more a Four Seasons type. Or the Union Square Café, when he feels like dressing down."

I looked sideways at the newcomers, who Pete was handing off to Sheila for seating. "*That's* Vincent Colby, huh?"

"In the flesh. And that's probably a good two-grand worth of fabric and cut."

Colby was not in mere Brooks Brothers. I made that beautifully assembled charcoal pin-striped affair as Armani, similar to one Velda had tried, unsuccessfully, to get me into.

I'd heard of this handsome young guy. Read about him (profiles in the Sunday *Times* and *New York Magazine*). Ivy League school (Harvard Business, wasn't it?). Prominent in the family brokerage firm (Colby, Daltree & Levine). Eminently eligible bachelor (dating society girls).

I asked Shannon, "Is that kid as upstanding as his rep?"

Shannon was watching as Sheila led Colby across the room, the two Wall Street big shots trailing along like litter bearers.

"Far as I know," Shannon said. "Like his old man, that 'kid' served in the Navy, made Lieutenant."

"Straight shooter all the way?"

His mouth twitched. "Some youthful indiscretions, I understand. No police record, but under-age records get expunged, particularly if you have connections." He sipped his highball. "Colby's guilty, all right—of being a rich Golden Boy, but that's about it."

"Far as you know."

"Far as I know, Mike."

Sheila was getting them seated in a booth at the bar area, across the dining room. Only Colby didn't sit down right away. He was standing there chatting with the redhead. She was smiling and trading talk in a friendly way. More of that going-nowhere flirtation? Or something else?

I said, "He sounds too good to be true."

"That's been my feeling," Shannon admitted. "I always felt like he was playing me."

"Playing you how, Casey?"

He twitched another sneer. "Too friendly. Too cooperative. Patronizing, like he was putting one over."

"How did you rub shoulders with the lad?"

"I had a couple of investigations that took me to the Colby firm."

"What kind of investigations?"

He didn't look at me while we talked. Suddenly it was like pulling teeth. He said, "A secretary there died of an overdose. A low-level employee was the victim of a hit-and-run."

"Fatal?"

Shannon nodded. "Vaguely suspicious but nothing came of either. Colby was in the lives of both parties. Was helpful to a fault."

Sheila was lingering, and Colby took her two hands in his and smiled and she smiled back, then peeled away. Could this privileged punk be the guy roughing her up? Maybe somebody needed to put the break in brokerage.

Colby was finally about to sit down, but maybe he felt our eyes on him, because he paused, spotted us, beamed and came over, navigating the sea of tables of diners like the Navy man he was.

He stood before our booth and half-nodded to each of us in turn, but reserved his dazzling white smile for Shannon, who was looking up at the man in Armani with a smile as rumpled as his own decidedly off-the-rack suit.

This was my first close look at the guy, and it revealed a male specimen who was almost too handsome, with long eyelashes and dark curly hair worn rather short and wet with product, giving him a Roman Emperor look. But was he Julius Caesar or Caligula? Either way, he sported a tan that said trips to warmer climes were not infrequent or maybe he just used a tanning bed somewhere. At home, maybe.

Colby leaned in and offered his hand to Shannon, who half-stood, as much as possible in the booth anyway, and accepted the proffered paw for a shake, then settled back down.

"So I'm guessing this is a retirement party?" Colby said, his voice mellow and smooth. He could become a TV or radio announcer if being a rich Wall Street heir didn't work out.

"*Pre*-retirement," Shannon said genially. You could never have discerned that the old copper had any suspicions or negative thoughts at all about the guy. Strictly friendly time.

"I recognize both of your partners in crime," the young man said, showing off those white teeth some more. His nods were more acknowledging this time around. "Sergeant Higgins. Detective Peters." The teeth and pretty eyes came to me and his smile settled in one cheek. "You're Mike Hammer, aren't you?"

"Guilty as charged."

Dark eyebrows rose above the long lashes. "That was some case you wrapped up a while back. Caused ripples from here to Europe. Stock market took a dive when those revelations about the CIA being infiltrated made the news."

I gave him a smile. A little one, not dazzling at all. "That wasn't my intention. To me he was just a bad guy, a very bad guy, who needed to be dealt with."

Colby's smile went damn near pixie-ish. "By which you mean… you shot him. Killed him."

I shrugged. "He had a gun. A little one. Mine was bigger."

The smile broadened in genuine amusement. "And here I thought size wasn't everything."

"It isn't. But it doesn't hurt."

"If it's big *enough* it does." He sighed, smiled again, no teeth now. "Well, gentlemen, I didn't mean to intrude. I just wanted to say hello to Casey here. Congratulate him on his retirement." He turned his eyes on Shannon. "See you later."

He flipped a casual wave and ambled across the room, graceful in a masculine way. Handsome devil, like Tony Curtis and George Hamilton had a kid. Women were looking at him the way men look at women.

"Why's he so friendly," I asked, "to a cop he encountered on a couple of suspicious-death inquiries? First name basis and everything. 'See you later?'"

Shannon said, "We go to the same gym."

I frowned. "I thought you went to Bing's, like me?"

A shrug. "I used to. I switched to the Solstice Fitness Center, few months ago."

I frowned deeper. "Over on Broadway?"

Shannon nodded.

"Isn't that a little pricey?"

Bigger shrug. "I got a deal on a membership. Have a personal trainer and everything. Just 'cause I'm retiring doesn't mean I want to grow a gut."

He kind of already had grown one, but I didn't say anything.

Our food came. Crisp cold salad with iceberg lettuce and garlic dressing. The rib-eyes thick and tender, mine blood-rare the way I like it. We shared two orders of Pete's legendary hash browns with onions, and the chow was such that conversation got mostly sidelined for a while.

I was keeping half an eye on Sheila and not just because she was worth at least that. On two occasions Colby got up and happy accidents let him come back into contact with her. Happily contrived accidents, I figured.

Once when he got up to go to the head, which took him past her station, that gave him an excuse to pause and jaw with her a while, on his way back to the booth.

Another time he joined her at the bar where she was chatting with the white-shirt, black-bowtie bartender, who was another good-looking guy in his late twenties or early thirties, but just maybe lacking the Colby kid's bank book. The Wall Street heir took her by the arm—not rough at all, and I was watching for that—and walked her over to one side and then they were talking in a serious way.

Not an argument. But not chit-chat or flirtation, either. These two knew each other. The bartender was taking this in, glaring at them as he filled orders. What the hell was that about?

We were having a round of after-dinner highballs as I watched Colby and the hostess discussing something near the bar again, and the bartender maybe resenting it. I wondered if the bartender was just a friend of Sheila's who maybe knew Colby had been treating her roughly, and was considering stepping in and doing something about it. In which case, hurrah for the bartender.

I said to Shannon, "I thought Colby dated the debutante crowd."

"He does. Sometimes."

"Not always?"

"He's been known to date models."

"The *Vogue* variety?"

Shannon sipped his highball. Shook his head. "More like *Playboy* and *Penthouse*. He parties at the Tube in Chelsea."

The Tube was more blue jeans than Armani, a trendy spot known for multiple lounges with such funky themes as an S & M dungeon, Victorian library, and a dance floor with cages, plus hot-and-cold-running cocaine.

After a final round of drinks, the little retirement get-together petered out, and Shannon and his two partners all took their leave, after fighting over who would take the check. Pat won. I hadn't made a bid, because I was always happy to see a cop pick up a check for a change.

Soon Pat and I were alone in the booth. Over in the bar area, the three stock brokers were having their own after-dinner drinks, and Colby had not invented any more excuses to bump into Sheila.

"Is it my imagination," I said to Pat, "or was something going on with Shannon?"

"What do you mean?"

"Well, he starts out kind of bitching about this Colby character. Then as I get to asking questions, suddenly I have to work to pry even tidbits of information out of him about the boy. And Casey Shannon going to a rich-guy, personal-trainer-type gym? What the shit? And the friendly way he talks to that 'Golden Boy,' and then how wary he seemed, and unfriendly toward him, when Colby wasn't standing in front of us?"

"Yeah," Pat said, "I picked up on that."

"So you're still a detective, then. Good to know. So what the hell do you make of it?"

Pat sucked in air and let it out again. "Feels like maybe he's doing some kind of undercover operation pertaining to Colby. Then when you got interested, he pulled back."

"You know something I don't?"

"I know plenty you don't, buddy." Then, with a shrug, Pat said, "Hey, I'm his boss and I sure as hell didn't assign anything like that."

I leaned in. "Could somebody above you have put something in motion?"

"Maybe," he said, with another shrug and a shake of his head, "but with a guy a few weeks out from retirement? Doesn't make sense."

"How about something personal? A case he wants to wrap up before he heads for the exit and pension land?"

"Possible. Possible." Pat gave me that wry, sly grin of his. "I *have* known certain assholes go off on private tears, now that you mention it."

"Screw you, buddy," I said with my own nasty grin.

As it happened, we almost followed Colby and his party out onto the sidewalk.

Colby was saying good night to his friends, and was just stepping into the street to jaywalk across the light eastbound traffic, apparently to his parked car, glancing back at them as he did with a smile and a wave. I'd already heard the squeal of tires from down the street, and the low-slung red vehicle came up so fast it might have materialized.

Seemed to have come from just down the block, though, so the sports car hadn't picked up much speed when it clipped Colby, who tumbled across the hood of the car, as the driver saw him and slowed, then picked speed back up when the man who'd been struck lay in a pile on the street.

I didn't get much of a look at the driver, but I saw a pony tail and it wasn't a woman—not unless she had a beard.

Pat was yelling at the fleeing vehicle, then got his little notebook out to jot down the license number, but I could see the plate was smeared with mud, so that was a non-starter.

Me, I was joining the two Wall Street gents in bending over their fallen friend, as the few cars out on the street right now were reducing speed and winding around us—nobody else stopping to help or offer witness info. People suck sometimes.

Colby, in his Burberry, was sitting up, holding his head with both hands, wincing, moaning.

"Vincent," said one of his friends, leaning in, "are you all right, man?"

The other friend said, "Can you get to your feet?"

Colby managed to nod and, with the help of both his companions, rose and hobbled over to the sidewalk, where a few pedestrians and some other diners from the restaurant were gathered for a gawk. The accident victim kept one hand on the side of his head.

"Bounced...bounced," the young man said. "Off the windshield. Shit, it hurts."

"We'll get you to the hospital," the first friend said, "right now."

That's when I noticed Sheila had emerged from the restaurant. She was standing there, agape, a hand over her mouth. She seemed about to go to Colby, but then—for some reason—stayed put. Still, she appeared on the verge of tears.

The bartender showed up behind her. His expression was hard to read, but not impossible. Amusement flicked on his lips. That was a hint of a smile, all right. And reacting with even a hint of satisfaction at the sight of somebody who's just been hit by a car, that isn't normal. That isn't typical. That sucked even more than usual for human behavior.

The bartender put a hand on her shoulder, supportive or pretending to be, and she patted the hand.

Was that redheaded hostess in the middle of two men? Such triangles can have their violent aspects. Women far less good-looking than Sheila Who's-it have stirred up a shitload of harm without meaning to.

Pat came up to the little group supporting Colby, falling in next to me, and held up his badge in its leather fold, saying, "I'm a police officer. Captain Chambers." He quickly took their names and jotted them in the notebook. Then he handed both Wall Street gents a card and asked for theirs. He would be in touch soon.

"I'll take care of reporting this," he told them. "Can anyone here say what make that vehicle was?"

The two gents shook their heads and Colby ignored the question, busy with his headache.

"Just a foreign job," I said. "Ferrari maybe."

One of the Wall Street guys, thinking it over, said, "Ferrari, yes—definitely."

The other one was flagging a cab, and then they were piling Colby carefully in back and they took off.

Pat, hands on his hips, watched the cab drive away. "That guy is lucky to be alive."

"Yeah."

"Five'll get you ten he's a concussion case."

"Yeah."

He frowned at me. "Something bugging you, Mike?"

"Don't know. Not sure."

"Come on, buddy. Spill."

I sighed. It was colder now and I snugged the trenchcoat collars up. "Just seemed a little...off to me."

Pat's grin was a scoffing thing. "Right. The guy intentionally stepped out in front of a speeding Jaguar, why? To get his jollies?"

"I don't know why. And don't know that he did. And that was a Ferrari."

He shook his head. "You have to be the most suspicious son of a bitch I ever knew."

"Really? How often am I wrong when I am?"

He didn't have an answer to that. He asked me if I needed a lift and I said yes. On the way to my place, I said damn near nothing. My mind was busy replaying what I'd seen, and wondering why it felt wrong somehow.

CHAPTER TWO

Velda and I lived in the same apartment building, but in separate digs on separate floors. We were a couple in every way except a diamond ring and a marriage certificate, but part of me was set in my bachelor ways with my own quirky mode of doing things.

For instance, I usually only spent the night with her on weekends. That was our wacko way of keeping work and play separate. And even then I would go down to my own pad to shower and shave, then make a breakfast for both of us, and she'd come down and join me.

Weekdays, she had her own schedule, heading to the office early, catching a bus. I would sometimes walk, sometimes run the ten blocks to the Hackard Building, changing out of sweats into fresh clothes I kept at the office. Certain mornings I worked out at Bing's Gym, taking a cab there and, later, to the office. It all had a rhythm, a regularity to it, that seemed random unless you were keeping track.

What never (or anyway rarely) changed was Velda getting in at the office on the eighth floor of the Hackard before me. She would get the coffee going (Dunkin' Donuts brand, the only way to fly) and organize any materials or matters that needed going over by either or both of us—client phone calls, insurance reports, letters, invoicing, bill-paying, appointments that took me out of the office, the routine stuff that doesn't make it into these write-ups.

My job was to pick up fresh Danish at the little restaurant around the corner. I would bring two, eat one and a half, and Velda would gorge herself on the remaining half. Like I told that redheaded hostess at Pete's the night before, my secretary/partner was watching her figure.

And what a figure.

This morning, like so many mornings when I came in through the pebbled glass door that said MICHAEL HAMMER INVESTIGATIONS, I was suspicious that Velda had heard my footfall in the hall and assumed the position, bending over to access a lower drawer of her file cabinet, presenting that world class fanny of hers for my inspection and delight. Her attire this morning was typical—a black pencil skirt and a pale blue silk blouse.

"Good morning, Mike," she said, without even looking.

"How do you know I'm not that guy who came in and crowned you not long ago," I said, depositing the bag of Danish on the little table under the window at left where the coffee maker bubbled. "He put you in the hospital, remember?"

She stood and, a file folder in hand, smiled at me as I climbed out of the Burberry (but not cashmere) coat and walked back toward the door to hang it and my Dobbs hat in the closet.

"Don't you remember, boss?" she replied smoothly. "You killed that son of a bitch."

She rarely used terms of endearment at work. Separating business and pleasure, like I said.

"I remember, doll," I said, "and it was a fucking pleasure."

I did use terms of endearment at the office.

I went over, got myself some coffee—she had a cup already poured—and doctored mine with milk and sugar. Then I put my Danish and a half on one paper plate and her half on the other, and delivered both to her desk, where she was heading with the folder.

Velda had come to work for me within a few months of my opening this office—in this very space; it had been remodeled but still looked like it was 1952. You could almost say the same about Velda. She was near my age but looked fifteen years younger. Maybe twenty. Guys half her years goggled at her in the street, and it didn't make me jealous, just proud.

She was tall, even in the flats she wore at work. Her raven hair was cut in a style-defying, shoulder-brushing pageboy that had auburn highlights in it now, her big brown eyes set off by light brown eye shadow, the dark long eyelashes needing no help from Maybelline, her lush lips glossed a sultry burgundy. That classical hourglass shape was supported by long legs, muscular in the dancer's sense, and full high breasts on loan from the young Jane Russell.

"You know what I love?" she asked.

"Me?"

She was gliding behind her desk, opposite the entry of an outer office just big enough to accommodate some reception chairs on either side and our little coffee and snacks table under the left-hand window. Behind her desk and to the left a little was the door to my inner sanctum.

"What I love," she said, nodding to the client's chair opposite her, "is reading something fresh and new and exciting about you in the paper. Something you haven't shared with me. You know how I adore surprises."

She was pushing this morning's *Daily News* at me, open to page three, already turned so that I could read it. After all, she already had.

The headline across the top of the tabloid page, the copy taking up a third of the page, was WALL STREET UP-AND-COMER STRUCK DOWN. Two photos of Vincent Colby—a close-up portrait shot and a candid of him and some society gal at a gala event—accompanied the article.

I set my coffee cup on Colby's puss. "I didn't have anything to do with that."

She wiggled a finger with a burgundy-painted nail at the paper. "You're an eyewitness, quoted and identified."

"Right. I'm that fabled innocent bystander you hear so much about."

She grunted a laugh, then reached for her half a Danish and nibbled on it like a mouse at cheese still in the trap. "And you're identified as, 'Michael Hammer, venerable private investigator whose numerous self-defense pleas in justifiable homicide cases have vexed the New York State court system for decades.'"

"That should drum up some business anyway," I said through a mouthful of pastry. "Venerable means older than shit, doesn't it?"

"Yes it does," she confirmed. "It also says the hit-and-run victim was seen earlier talking to you and a certain captain of Homicide at the restaurant. What about?"

She was pissed—mildly pissed, but still pissed—because I

hadn't called her last night or first thing this morning to fill her in. She is understanding in ways I could expect no woman ever to be with me, but reading about me in the paper, finding out about something in that fashion and not directly from me, frosted her tail but good.

So I filled her in.

No heat was coming off her at all now, other than what was generated by those good looks that I never got used to or took for granted.

"You really were just a witness," she said, mildly surprised. "An innocent bystander."

"Innocent as a new-born babe, that's me." I leaned back in the chair, coffee cup in hand. "But that doesn't mean I'm not on the spot."

"It doesn't?" She had this ability to suggest a frown without wrinkling her forehead much, if at all; one of her beauty maintenance secrets. "Why not?"

"Hit-and-run is a crime."

"Let me write that down."

"It's a crime, and I was at the scene. Furthermore, I was observed talking to the victim, in the company of that 'certain' captain of the Homicide Division. You may have met him—Patrick Chambers?"

"I believe we have met, yes," she said archly. "So how does any of that put you on the spot?"

"Somebody important almost got killed, under my nose. I will be expected to do something about it, else look like a chump."

Her smile would have been as enigmatic as the Mona Lisa's

if Da Vinci had put some smugness in the picture. "You have a rather rarefied opinion of yourself, Mr. Hammer. This isn't the old days when you were filling the tabloids so colorfully—mostly red."

I gestured with my cup toward the paper. "The Penta thing got play."

"Yes, and after you killed that bastard, both the *News* and the *Post* did those nice retrospectives about your 'wild exploits' back in the days of Howdy Doody and Milton Berle. You know what that makes you?"

"A celebrity?"

"Nostalgia." She tapped the page three. "Nobody expects you to solve this. Anyway, it's an accident. Not attempted murder."

"We don't know that."

She studied me. Velda had me down so well, she didn't have to study long. She put a dozen words of question into just one: "What?"

I sipped the coffee. "Something's off about it."

"About the hit-and-run?"

"Yeah."

"The *News* says young Colby narrowly escaped death. Do you have any reason to think somebody targeted him for a kill? Are you thinking you may have a well-heeled client on the hook? You're not usually one for ambulance chasing."

"Maybe I'm Ferrari chasing."

The big brown eyes narrowed. "You know, Mike—Mr. Wall Street Hotshot's reputation is pretty darn stellar. Colby is generally thought, around town, to be a good guy. Attends, and even occasionally throws, charity events. That AIDS benefit on

Broadway last month? That was him."

I sighed. Shook my head. "Truth, kitten? Something about that accident stinks. It had a staged look, a phony feel."

She turned her head and looked at me sideways. "You mean faked?"

"I don't know what I mean, frankly. He got hit all right, and his two Wall Street cronies hauled him off to the hospital. Maybe staged in the sense that it was no hit-and-run accident, but a murder attempt. I told you Casey Shannon mentioned two suspicious deaths Colby was at least on the fringes of."

"And you think Shannon may've been investigating him, related to one or more of those deaths? Fine. So talk to Shannon."

I shook my head. "If he's working under deep cover for somebody over Pat's head, Casey won't give me a glimmer. Or if it's personal, he'll keep that close to his vest. No, I think the one to talk to is Vincent Colby."

That widened her eyes. "If he's up to *having* visitors."

"If he isn't," I said, getting to my feet, "I'll talk to his doctors. If he's suffered some injuries, then maybe I'm all wet about that thing being staged. And he may need help at that."

I was in my hat and coat at the door when she called out to me, still at her desk.

"Thanks for dropping by," she said.

I had been to Bellevue Hospital many times, but never—as some might imagine—so I could be admitted to the mental ward. Still, you could go mad in certain quarters of the place. You could get spit on by prisoners in cuffs and orange jammies as you passed by, and you could pause to watch a dope addict slug a doc and make a break for it while nurses and guards hustled after him to save their jobs. You could glance through doors into featureless rooms where the homeless had finally found a place to die, or others where addicts were shrieking and writhing. Down the hall, an undocumented Haitian might be dying of AIDS, looking like something out of a zombie flick. Yes, you could drive yourself stark staring nuts without trying at all in the lower reaches of the city's flagship hospital.

But I was not in a circle of hospital hell on this visit. I was headed to an upper floor in a wing funded by the likes of Vincent Colby's family. I'd stopped in the First Avenue lobby at the information desk to pick up a visitor's pass. I described myself as a friend and that's all it took. Visiting hours were eight to eight, and it was just after nine a.m. now.

With my hat on and my coat over my sleeve, I stepped onto an elevator, and when I stepped off, I just about ran headlong into Sheila, the curvy redheaded hostess from Pete's Chophouse.

You might figure she wouldn't look as good this time of morning, making a hospital visit, and it's true the fluorescent lighting wasn't as flattering as the low-key illumination at the supper club. But the green-eyed beauty—in a denim jacket, pink sweater and jeans today—had the same lovely face with the Bardot mouth, now with blush on her cheeks and watermelon eye shadow to make her seem younger and more in tune with her generation's style than last night's green evening dress when she was playing hostess to dinosaurs like me.

One touch remained the same: she still had flesh-colored make-up applied to hide that shiner some son of a bitch gave her.

"Mike!" she said.

"Sheila. Am I that frightening?"

She smiled, laughed a little. "No, it's just...always funny to run into somebody in another context, y'know? I never saw you anywhere but Pete's. Or in the paper or on the TV news."

I gave her half a smile. "I know what you mean. For example, I've known you for several years, but I never caught your last name."

"It's Ryan." She gestured down the hall. "Are you here to...?"

Nodding, I said, "Stop by to see how Mr. Colby's doing. I saw that hit-and-run go down, y'know. I take it that's why you're here?"

"It is."

I gestured to a nearby nook where a patient's relatives and friends could sit and wait and read ancient magazines. "Got a minute?"

"Sure."

We shared a two-seater couch.

I asked, "How's the patient doing?"

She shrugged. "A little groggy from the meds, but I think he's doing all right. A doctor's in with him now. You're a friend of Vincent's?"

"Not really. Just met him last night. He stopped by our booth to say hello to Casey Shannon, who we were throwing a little retirement party for, as you probably picked up on."

"Oh yes, the 'Wall Street Cop.'" Her eyes narrowed. "Is he some kind of financial expert or something?"

"Hell no, just a copper who worked that part of town and, in so doing, got to know some of the Stock Market crowd." I gave her the whole smile now, but didn't push it. "I'm going to ask you a nosy, none-of-my-business question."

Her head bobbed back and her smile got just a little wary. "You are, huh?"

I shrugged. "I'm a professional snooper by trade. You know that. And I witnessed a crime last night. So I can't help myself. I get interested."

Sheila returned the shrug. "I guess that makes sense."

"Are you two an item, Ms. Ryan?"

She shook her head. "No, we're just...friendly acquaintances?"

"Are you asking me?"

"No, of course not. I just meant...I know him from the restaurant. He's a patron, a frequent one." Her shrug only involved one shoulder. "He's good-looking, very smooth, charming, and he likes to joke around with me. Just a fun flirt. Nothing more."

"Maybe. But I couldn't help noticing he seemed more than just casually interested in you."

Her mouth smiled but her forehead frowned. "You *are* a snoop, aren't you?"

"Definitely. Has Colby ever asked you out?"

"No! We're just friends. Friendly."

"Yet you're here visiting him at the hospital, first thing in the morning."

She leaned toward me, as if speaking to a backward child. "Mr. Hammer, I know him from the restaurant. He got hit by a *car* outside that restaurant! I was just being...polite. Nice."

"Did your boss ask you to stop by on the restaurant's behalf?"

"No. I just thought it was...you know, the right thing to do."

She stood. "Mr. Hammer, I have a hair stylist appointment to get to, if you don't mind."

I stopped her, gently, with a hand at her elbow. "Ms. Ryan... Sheila. Was Colby responsible for that black eye you're trying, not very well, to hide?"

The green eyes flashed down at me. "No! Really, Mr. Hammer. You're out of line now. I told you, we are not...how did you so quaintly put it? An 'item.' Anyway, I'm...never mind."

"You're what?"

"I'm *already* in a relationship."

I got to my feet and now I was looking down at her and her puffy eye. "With somebody *else* who gave you that mouse, you mean? What, that bartender? You promised me last night you were breaking it off with your abusive boy friend, I just figured it might be Colby."

Her teeth were clenched; they were small and white and pretty. "You were right the first time."

"I was?"

"This is none of your fucking business!"

She marched off quickly to the elevator and stood there, steaming a little, while she waited for the car.

I sat back down and frowned and tried to figure out why the back of my neck was tingling. This really was none of my business, fucking or otherwise. I had no dog in this fight. No client, no money riding.

When had that ever stopped me?

The girl was gone, but a doctor was exiting a room just down the hall, pausing to make some clipboard notes. I got up and made it down there in time to confirm that he'd emerged from the room whose number identified it as Colby's, the door to which was closed.

"Excuse me, doctor," I said, when he'd finished his notations and was about to resume his duties, and noticed my presence for the first time. His name badge said DR. MARTIN CORNELL. He was about forty with short dark hair, a trim matching beard and alert but distant brown eyes behind wireframe glasses.

"Yes?" he said, with as much patience as could be expected from a man as busy as he no doubt was.

"I'm a friend of Mr. Colby's," I asked. "Would I be out of line asking how he's doing?"

He thought about that for a moment, then apparently decided sharing his patient's condition would do no harm. "He suffered some bruises. Considering the circumstances, he's a lucky man indeed."

"Great to hear. I was at the scene."

"Were you?"

"Yes, and he was complaining about a head injury, right after the incident. That's what was worrying me. Vince and I go way back, you see."

That seemed to mildly amuse the doctor. "Well, you must go back a ways, if you call him 'Vince.'"

"Oh?"

"He made it clear to me, in no uncertain terms, that he prefers to be called Vincent."

I grinned. "Yeah, I don't let him get away with that crap. When I knew him, we called him a lot worse than 'Vince.' So is it a concussion, or...?"

"Mr. Colby has all the common symptoms of a concussion, yes—headache, dizziness, coordination problems, he's had some nausea and vomiting, blurred vision, sensitivity to light, sensitivity to noise, and so on."

"How serious is it?"

He flipped a hand. "Oh, we'll be releasing him later today. The effects of concussion are usually temporary, recovery complete. I'm only concerned about…well, nothing."

"Doctor. Please. Maybe I can help."

He thought about that, then surprised me by putting a supportive hand on my shoulder. "I don't know Mr. Colby. He was not my patient before today. But you should be aware—so that you're not alarmed or react in a way that would disturb him— that your friend may be suffering from one of the less frequent effects of concussion."

"What's that?"

"Behavior or personality changes."

"Really."

"Can you tell me…what is your name?"

"Hammer."

"Can you tell me, Mr. Hammer—is Mr. Colby usually known to…fly easily off the handle, let's say?"

"No. He's known to be quite self-composed." At least that was my understanding.

One eyebrow rose above the wireframes. "Well, right now he's showing some definite ill temper. Not that 'ill temper' is a common diagnosis of mine. But it's evidenced here. His father came by earlier—his mother is deceased, I understand—and I informed the older Mr. Colby of this. But he'd already witnessed as much, and obviously seemed disturbed by it…" He sighed, lifted both eyebrows this time, then said, "You can see him now."

"Thank you, Dr. Cornell."

He went off and I went in.

The room was private, not surprisingly, and spacious. Some flowers, quite a few really, had already made their way here, lining a windowsill and finding room on a nightstand. Vincent Colby wasn't hooked up to any hanging bottles with tubes stuck in him or anything, and he was propped up, casually watching CNN on the high-mounted TV.

"Yes?" he said, squinting at me as I stood at the half-open door.

"Mike Hammer, Mr. Colby. We met last night at Pete's. I was just checking to see how you're doing. I saw that red hot rod try to make a speed bump out of you."

He smiled, gave me a curled-fingered gesture. "Sorry, I didn't recognize you—vision's a little fouled up…it's like I'm looking through dirty glasses. Come in, Mike. And Mr. Colby is my father—*I'm* Vincent."

I walked to his bedside. He looked much the same, tan and fit, though the curly hair was a dry dark tangle now. He had a reddish-blue hematoma on his forehead, over his left eye.

"My secretary," I said, "is accusing me of ambulance chasing, coming around here. But really it's just my damn curiosity getting the best of me. As usual."

He was squinting at me again, or maybe that was a wince. "What got you curious? It was an accident, wasn't it? Not that I wouldn't like to get a *hold* of that son of a bitch!"

He demonstrated with clawed hands. And the eyes weren't squinting now.

"Yeah," I said with a grin, "I been there. You may have heard that I'm kind of known for settling grudges in my own way."

He smiled. "Are they exaggerating?"

"Understating. Look, I'm told I have a nose for certain things—murder, for example."

"I don't seem to be dead, Mike."

"Well, this snout of mine can also sniff out *attempted* murder. Do you have anybody in your life who might like to see you turned into a stain on the pavement?"

He risked a small shrug. "I suppose I have enemies. Work and private life alike. But not *that* kind of enemy. No. Not at all."

"Well. You think about it. Just don't think yourself into an even worse headache. But if there's something I can do for you, say the word. I can leave a card if you like."

He grinned; even in this lighting, it was dazzling. "Are you *sure* you aren't ambulance chasing?"

I grinned back. "Pretty sure. You mind if I ask you something?"

"Won't know till you do."

"Out in the hall, I ran into the hostess from Pete's—Sheila Ryan. Are you two…anything?"

He started to shake his head and then the pain of that stopped him. "No. We're just pals. I'm a regular and she's a cute kid. Joke around. Flirt. You know how it is."

I worked up a lascivious grin. "I just figured, guy like you, good-looking, with all that bread, and here she's just working at a mid-range restaurant…"

He frowned. "Figured what?"

"I don't know. That she might be on the make. I know *I* wouldn't be immune to that."

"To what?"

"That ripe a piece of tail."

Colby jerked upright and both of his hands made fists out of themselves. "Watch what you say, Hammer! Or I'll feed you that tough-guy reputation one tooth at a time!" He grabbed my card off the nightstand and flipped it at me. "Stick that up your ass, you fucking prick!"

I raised both hands. "No offense meant."

I slipped out into the hall, shutting the door behind me, grinning to myself.

"Thought so," I said.

CHAPTER THREE

The offices of Colby, Daltree & Levine, near Wall Street, took up the thirty-seventh floor of a glass and concrete tower, just another giant tombstone marking, some would say, the graveyard that was Manhattan's Financial District—a place where at times it seemed that integrity had gone to die.

Just two years ago the Wall Street boom had gone bust, thanks to corporate raiders, leveraged buyouts, junk bonds, and especially insider trading, where high finance had become street corner deals where cash-filled suitcases were passed from one dirty white-collar hand to another.

Though several weeks had passed, I'd been summoned to the Colby firm, retaining enough curiosity about that hit-and-run I'd witnessed to accept the invitation with neither hesitation nor query.

After taking a cab from the Hackard Building, I signed in at the Liberty Exchange lobby with a uniformed guy about my age who seemed even more surprised than I did to find my name on the approved list.

I went on up.

Soon I was strolling down one of several aisles that separated rows of jammed-together desks, making my way through this many-windowed Yuppie warren as unnoticed as a towel attendant at a Turkish bath. Computer monitors cast their aquarium-green glow on at least one hundred brokers and sales assistants (almost exclusively male, in phone headsets and suspenders and no jacket), nobody ever seeming to pause to take in a panoramic harbor view that started at the Brooklyn Bridge and extended to Governors Island.

They were working the phones, making cold call after cold call, colder than the gray sky they were ignoring out all those windows as they projected confidence and success in this vast, soulless, drop-ceilinged boiler room, worker bees basking in the same kind of fluorescent lighting that Bellevue dispensed to its patients.

On the west side of the floor was a row of glassed-in offices penning up slightly older individuals with designer suspenders and two-hundred-buck haircuts.

These offices had Danish modern furniture and a couple of green-glow monitors on separate low-slung tables behind desks the size of knocked-over refrigerators with surfaces that somehow managed to be cluttered and orderly at the same time. I wandered in that direction, all the phone chatter around me like the buzzing of stirred-up hornets.

As I neared the row of window-walled workstations, a familiar face behind the glass of the larger central office landed on mine. Vincent (for heaven's sake, don't call him Vince) was on the phone, not surprisingly, and—in addition to the two behind him—he had an extra computer monitor right on his desk. Like his minions, he was in shirt sleeves and suspenders, but his probably cost plenty more.

That was the world we lived in now. Designer suspenders.

Young Colby frowned at me. It was damn near a scowl.

I smiled a little, put a touch of smirk in it. Gave him a tiny tickle-the-air wave, like I'd spotted a child I knew playing in a park. Well, hadn't I?

I took a right to go down a short hallway tucked behind a wall of photocopy machines. Here were offices you couldn't see into, with various executive vice presidents in them, assuming their doors weren't lying – the older breed of execs like those who'd accompanied young Colby to Pete's Chophouse. The hall led to a receptionist—a forty-something, severe but beautiful brunette in a gray tailored suit, cream-color silk blouse, and black-framed mannish glasses. She had cheekbones that could cut glass.

Despite Velda's attempts to make a respectable-looking man of business out of me, my non-cashmere Burberry, Dobbs hat-in-hand, and Today's Man threads failed to impress.

She asked, "May I help you?" like a floorwalker to a shoplifter. Her nameplate said Ms. Stern. Really.

"Your boss is expecting me. Mike Hammer."

Her manner shifted. She'd been given that name, it was on *her* list too; but the moniker itself had meant nothing to her. There was a time…

"May I take your coat and hat?" she asked, butter wouldn't melt.

I nodded, she rose, and I gave them to her.

"Now, if you'll take a seat," she said, squeezing out a smile, gesturing to the little row of chairs, "it will be just a few moments."

In the weeks that had passed since my visit to Vincent Colby at Bellevue, my life—and business—had gone on. The peculiarities of the hit-and-run at Pete's, and what I was now taking for a love triangle between Colby, Sheila Ryan and whatever that bartender's name was, continued to linger. And linger for no good reason, as Velda would remind me (ever more impatient) whenever I brought it up.

Then this morning Vincent Colby's father had called the offices of Michael Hammer Investigations—not this secretary or receptionist, whichever Ms. Stern was, but Vance Colby himself, the president of the firm. Velda had been suitably impressed, so my ice queen here wasn't the first female today to underestimate me.

And, as promised, in a manner of moments, I was ushered in to a world apart from that bustling boiler room out there. This chamber, with not a computer monitor in sight, might have been a Financial District office fifty years ago. The walls were dark lush wood with gleaming parquet flooring and an occasional Oriental carpet under a high, elaborately-molded ceiling—no acoustic tiles here.

The furnishings were fine wood with plush upholstery, and framed landscapes spruced up the palatial walls—none of this modern art nonsense that had only been around for a hundred years or so. A fireplace big enough to accommodate a couple of St. Nicks and their bags of goodies was overseen by a huge gilt-framed standing portrait of a middle-aged man in formal attire, circa 1920—the late Vernon P. Colby (a nameplate boldly read), who resembled a more severe, dignified but every bit as handsome version of his grandson Vincent.

The man who came trundling around a mahogany desk, which

was smaller than a tank but not much, had similar facial features to his son and that of his own gilt-framed father. But this was a smaller man, made even more so by the vastness of the chamber, somewhat portly—no matter how hard his well-tailored charcoal pinstripe suit tried to conceal it. His silver hair lay in curls like his son's, that Roman Emperor effect again, but his well-grooved face was home to a skinny salt-and-pepper mustache, while his gilt-framed father and window-enclosed son were clean shaven.

"Mr. Hammer," Vance Colby said, his hand extended even before he'd reached me, his voice mellow like his son's, "you're kind to respond to my entreaty so quickly."

"Sure," I said, as we shook. His hand was small but his grip large. "But you didn't indicate the nature of your, uh, entreaty."

"Sit, sit, sir. Please."

He was gesturing to a pair of two-seater couches facing each other by the hearth, a modest gas fire going, the cold snap out in the real world making it appropriate. The low-slung coffee table between us had a gleaming pot of its namesake waiting on a silver tray with china cups to be filled.

"Coffee?" he asked, as if the thought had just occurred to him. "Thanks."

He poured, then told me to help myself to cream and sugar, which I did.

As he settled back on the couch, a steaming cup in hand, my host said, "I'm of an age, Mr. Hammer, to know of you first-hand, from your newspaper exploits."

That was second-hand, really, but I just said, "I'm of an age to have had them. Might I ask, sir..." His formality was catching.

"…if you mean that as a compliment, or just an observation?"

"A compliment, definitely," Vance Colby said, sitting forward, putting the coffee cup on a coaster on the glass top between us. He grinned and it seemed a little forced. "You know, somehow I always felt that we had a lot in common."

Yeah, I was just thinking that.

But what I said was, "How's that, Mr. Colby?"

He flipped a hand. "Well, politically, for instance."

I grunted a laugh. "Not unless you haven't voted for twenty years, either."

That widened his eyes, which were faded blue and not the pretty eyes of his son—that must have been Vincent's mother's DNA.

"Really, Mr. Hammer? A man with your strong opinions doesn't *vote*? Why ever not?"

"It only encourages them." I sat forward. "Sir, I'm going to guess you already have a big-ticket private security company handling both your business and your home. And we only have two licensed investigators in my firm, including my secretary. We're very good, but we're a staff of two."

He was nodding. "Understood."

I sat back. "And even if you don't already have a security outfit, I'm not an appropriate choice for your needs."

He sat back as well. Folded his arms. Some shrewdness came into his voice, which was a relief, because I had not been impressed so far. "You already know why you're here, don't you, Mike? If I may address you that way."

"Sure, if I can call you 'Vance.'" I sipped my coffee, which was world-class, like Juan Valdez himself had delivered it on his burro. "I get uncomfortable when I'm on a first-name basis with somebody who expects a 'mister' out of me in return."

He chuckled at that. "Of course. Obviously, this is about my son."

"Yeah, we exchanged greetings when I got here." Sort of. "You must be glad to have him back here at work."

Vance nodded, but seemed distracted. "Vincent was only in the hospital overnight, but, uh…before we go any further, I'd like to get you on retainer. Make this official. What would you say to $1,000?"

"Yippee?"

A grin blossomed, unforced this time. "I've taken the liberty," he said, and reached in a jacket pocket for a check fold. He tore the check out and handed it to me—he'd made it out in advance, and somehow I just knew he'd used a fountain pen. Probably a Mont Blanc.

But I raised a traffic-cop palm with one hand, the check drooping from my other.

"Is there a problem?" he asked, frowning, confused.

"A technicality. I work through an attorney. You become his client and that grants us the attorney/client confidentiality privilege."

His eyebrows went up and so did the corners of his smile. "Very wise, Mr. Hammer."

"My terms are $250 a day, the retainer my minimum. You cover expenses. My secretary will give you a detailed accounting at the wrap-up."

A hand flicked the air, as if shooing a fly. "Let's call it $1,000 a day, bump the retainer to $10,000, and you cover your own expenses."

"Sure." Having a rich client already had its benefits. "Unless there's out-of-state travel. That you'll cover."

"Certainly."

I carried a small stack of my attorney's cards in my wallet and got one out and handed it to him. Then my host rose, went to his mahogany monster of a desk, and filled out a new check (with a fountain pen), crumpling the old one and tossing it in a mahogany wastebasket. This chamber was an office, after all.

When I had the ten grand tucked away, I said, "Now we can talk. If your son is back at work, after such a short hospital stay, what's the problem?"

Seated across from me again, he leaned forward, hands folded and draped between his legs. He had a look of parental concern that every working private investigator knows too well.

"Mr. Hammer," Vance began, and sighed, and was searching for words when the words of someone else interrupted, loudly.

"*What the hell is* he *doing here?*"

The door behind me slammed as Vincent Colby entered, stalked across an Oriental carpet, talking to us as he approached, his face flushed, his eyes narrowed, brow furrowed, fists tight.

The father looked up as the son towered. "Son, I'm engaging Mr. Hammer here to find the offender."

Colby's fists went to his waist as he positioned himself at the end of the coffee table, his back to the fire, standing there like a demented Superman. "The 'offender'? You mean the son of a bitch who ran me *down*? *That* offender?"

"Yes," his father said calmly. "The driver."

Young Colby turned toward me. He stuck out a forefinger in my direction, more casual than accusing, as if at a zoo identifying which chimp threw monkey shit at him.

"I don't *like* this person," he blustered. "I don't like him one little bit."

He was twice as loud as necessary and he began to pace.

"Hammer said *offensive* things about someone I care *deeply* about, and he's lucky I didn't break him in half, then and there." Finally his eyes landed on me and his upper lip curled back. "But it's just not my *habit* to abuse the *elderly*."

I crossed my arms, and put my right ankle on my left knee as I took it all in expressionlessly. A comment or a grin from me would just make this worse. Nothing to do but wait it out.

"*I* will find the 'offender,'" young Colby said. "I have a good idea what happened, and who is responsible! And if I'm wrong, I know where to start after *that*."

"Son…"

Now he pointed at his father and it *was* accusatory. "*You* shut-up. Shut-up and stay out of my life, old man! You interfere in my private affairs and I will walk out of here and leave you to pick up the pieces." He turned to me again. "This old fool hasn't done a *thing* for this firm for ten years! The ancient mariner here has no *idea* what it takes to run a company like this, in this day and age! I doubt he knows how to *turn on* a computer!"

I knew. Velda had taught me.

Colby lurched forward and his father, still seated, backed away, frightened, as his son's fist came down, and I was poised to go for the raving ranter myself; but the base of the blow was meant for the table, and it connected, making everything on that coffee table jump.

Then Vincent Colby stormed out and slammed the door behind him.

We sat in silence for a while broken only by the gentle lapping of flames. Fortunately my coffee cup had been in my hand and not on the coffee table. I took a drink. Vance Colby had a hand over his face and was doing his best not to sob. His best wasn't enough.

I waited.

Soon he was dabbing at his face with a handkerchief. "I…I apologize, Mr. Hammer."

I smiled at him, just a gentle thing. "Mike, remember? Families are tough sometimes."

The smaller Colby gestured with both hands, as if balancing two objects. "That's just the thing! We've always been *close*, Vincent and I. Always. His mother died when he was seven and we've been best friends ever since. Never a harsh word between us. Until…"

I frowned. "Until the accident?"

He nodded. "Yes. I am assured by the medical experts that my son will fully recover, but…it may take time. Vincent is on medication and he is seeing a psychiatrist on a daily basis. So far it's…frankly, it's not doing any good." He swallowed. "But it's early. It's early yet."

"Has there been an impact on his work?"

His shrug was elaborate. "Vincent's working only half days— seeing the shrink in the afternoons, sometimes his physician, as well. There are…occasional explosions of temper. He's always been a charmer where the staff is concerned—a bit manipulative perhaps, but that's not a bad thing in this game. He has not, at least not as yet, evinced any signs of violent behavior."

My eyes got big as I pointed to the door Vincent had stormed through minutes ago. "What the hell would you call that?"

He lifted a hand. "No signs of *physical* violence, I should say. He's been short with his people, and lost it with them, and they understand, but it shakes them. It's so unlike him. He's been such a great boss to them. He also…oh, Mr. Hammer. This is hard."

"I know, sir. Go on."

Vance swallowed thickly. "When I get home tonight, one of two things will happen. Either Vincent will not remember any of this…amnesiac bouts can come with certain concussion cases, I have been told…or he may break down and cry and apologize. I am not generally a demonstrative man, Mr. Hammer, but I will hold my grown son in my arms. Hold him like a baby."

And he began to weep.

I went over and sat next to him. Put a hand on his shoulder. It made me uncomfortable as hell, but I did it. Maybe it was the ten grand in my pocket. Maybe I'm a human being after all, not that being one is anything to brag about.

"Your son is correct, I take it," I said, when he had composed himself, still sitting next to him, "that you want me find the hit-and-run driver."

He nodded. "I do not feel the police have done nearly a thorough enough job on what is to them, I'm sure, just a routine hit-and-run. They have very little to go on, admittedly. But I fear they've dismissed this, or at least downplayed it, due to a victim who was not badly hurt."

I shook my head. "You're not helpless in this. Someone like you could make noise. You could make it known that Vincent's injury was anything but 'routine.'"

He turned to me alarmed. "That kind of publicity would have

a *terrible* negative effect on this business! Daltree and Levine, the two partners of mine on our masthead, are deceased, and I am semi-retired. My son is the moving force behind our operation. I do not want his condition getting out. It would compromise the firm horribly."

"Okay." I got up and resumed my seat opposite him. "I get that."

Slumped, hands clasped, he stared at the floor. "Also, I feel there's a chance that something more might be behind this."

"You think someone might have been trying to kill Vincent."

He looked at me, his eyes hard now. "I do. My son has made enemies in business – he can be ruthless, which is necessary in this business. And you heard him talk about his own suspicions, though I'm afraid I have my doubts—that may be delusional behavior, another concussion symptom. But just the same, I'm already exploring that possibility."

"In what way?"

"As you surmised, I employ a major security firm."

He mentioned the outfit by name and I nodded, said they did good work. Assured him, on that score, they would do better than I could.

"So if this is related to business," Vance Colby said, "we'll assume they will find out. But if it's a *personal* matter...*you* will find out. Is that agreeable?"

"It is. Sir..."

"Vance. Please."

"Vance, your son may be involved in a love triangle of sorts, which provides me with an immediate avenue to go down."

His eyes tightened. "I knew nothing of that. Had no idea."

"I only have a vague sense of it myself, but it's a start. Is there anything else you can think of? I make no judgment when I ask this, but could he have been involved in drugs? Or any other illegal activity that would put him in contact with criminal elements?"

The father shook his head, firmly. "No drugs, certainly. He is something of a health enthusiast. Played rugby at Harvard. Lots of raw vegetables in his diet, very limited intake of red meat. Vitamins. Works out at home in our exercise room. Doesn't smoke. Very little drinking."

"What's he normally like? His personality, I mean. His temperament."

"In work my son walks a line between being conservative and, as I said, reckless—I'd generally call him moderate, but he will take a risk, if he feels it's called for. He has always been a deliberate boy. Maintains control. Which is why it's so terribly disturbing to see him fly off the handle, and go into such an erratic, violent tailspin."

"What exactly do you expect of me?"

"Find the person driving that red sports car."

"And what?"

He held up two hands, palms out, as if in surrender. "I'll leave that to your discretion. If this was truly an accident, turn the individual over to the police. If it does turn out to be someone striking out at Vincent, personally—if that incident was a *murder* attempt, not an accident…or if the man turns out to have been a drunk driver…use your own judgment."

I leaned forward. I spoke very quietly.

"Vance, I want no misunderstanding here. Despite my reputation, you're hiring an investigator, not a vigilante." I gestured around me. "Even with all this, you don't have enough money to hire me to kill someone, or even knock them around. I'm not a hired killer. Not a thug. No matter what some people believe."

"What if someone were to pull a gun on you?"

"I'd shoot them, of course."

He smiled. "That's good enough for me, Mike."

CHAPTER FOUR

You can drink till four a.m. in Manhattan, but some restaurants with bars set their own time for last call. Pete's Chophouse was one of those, which was where Velda and I headed for a late-night supper after taking in *Ain't Misbehavin'* at the Ambassador Theatre. There were plenty of places closer to grab a bite and a brew, but as usual I had a hidden agenda.

After a warm greeting from Pete in his shiny tux and suspiciously black hair and mustache, I deposited my coat and hat with the check-stand blonde. The lovely Sheila, in another green gown, nicely low-cut tonight, complimented Velda on her oversized black blazer and white turtleneck, then acceded to my request for seating in the bar area. The green-eyed redhead escorted us there with a smile and not a word about my last visit to the restaurant or to our previous, ultimately tense encounter at Bellevue. She still had an eye swollen up but camouflaged with cosmetics.

On a weeknight, at around a quarter till eleven, the old-fashioned, less-than-spacious supper club was sparsely populated, the not-too-smoky ambience going well with the low lighting.

Velda had a small chef's salad and I put away a rare steak

sandwich and fries, and a couple of Miller Lites. We took our time, and in low tones discussed the Colby job, and a job is what it was now that we had deposited the old man's check for ten grand. We kept our voices low while Sinatra, Dino, and Davis sang to us from the sound system.

"I'm still not sure," Velda said, "what it is you think we can do that the Motor Vehicle boys and girls can't do better."

"Maybe nothing. But we only have *one* hit-and-run to look into. Plus, there are aspects of this thing that they don't know about."

She was nodding. "Colby's mental state post-concussion, you mean."

I nodded back. "That, and the cast of players hugging the periphery."

She bobbed her head almost imperceptibly toward the bar. "Like that kid back there mixing drinks?"

We were both old enough to call anybody under forty a "kid," even if Velda's looks still made her a babe.

"Like him," I agreed. "He seems to know who I am, or anyway my face rings a bell."

"You're a regular here or nearly so. Maybe that's why."

I shook my head. "No, I never saw him before that night when Colby got clipped by the Ferrari. He might have noticed me when I went out into the street to see if Colby's Wall Street cronies needed help hauling their pal's ass to shore."

The bartender in his black bowtie and white shirt was glancing our way now and then with the kind of blank look that in a bartender reads as a scowl. He had a few filled stools to tend to—for cliff dwellers around here this was a neighborhood bar—and was going through the usual routine of making drinks to fill waitress orders, cleaning glasses, and wiping down areas after a customer exited. It was just that he seemed more interested in Velda and me than he did his work.

"Maybe he just digs older dolls," I said to her with a shrug.

She kicked me under the table. Gently. Fairly gently.

After sipping her Miller Lite, which they had on tap, she said, "You can't really suspect a bartender who's, what? Twenty-eight, thirty? Of having a friend with a Ferrari who he hired or talked into trying to run down his competition with that redhead."

"I don't rule anything out. And I suppose it's worth noting that Ms. Ryan, over there manning her post...and with that shape, 'manning' doesn't seem like the right word, does it? Don't you kick me again or I'll kick back. Anyway, it's worth noting that she denies being involved with Vincent Colby, and appears to be involved with this specimen...and she won't even admit that one of her male harem gave her that shiner."

"Which she still has to cover up with concealer," Velda said, "assuming you're enough of a detective to have noticed that when she seated us."

"I'm not only enough of a detective to've noticed that," I said, and sipped Miller, "I also noticed it was the other eye this time."

Don't be impressed. Velda couldn't have copped to that, not having seen Sheila with that other black eye, and only knowing about it second-hand from me.

"It *has* been a couple of weeks," Velda said, her own lovely eyes narrowing. "Plenty of time for that first mouse to stop squawking."

Pete rolled over to our booth with a big smile, leaning in to see how we were doing.

"Join us for a moment," I said.

He glanced around, saw nothing needing his attention, and slid in on Velda's side of the booth.

"It's good to see you again, Mike, so soon. Been too long between visits. I can't promise you one as memorable as last time, though!"

"Well, that's fine by me," I said. "But Velda and I are here for more than a late-night snack, good as that steak sandwich was. This is actually business."

"How so?"

I was keeping my voice down, way down, Sinatra providing cover. "I'm looking into that hit-and-run," I said, "working for young Colby's father."

My client had given me permission to drop his name if I felt that would help, which with somebody like Pete it did.

I continued: "Vincent Colby himself isn't pleased to have me poking in, but that can't be helped."

Pete was frowning; he didn't seem thrilled that this was turning out to be more than host/patron happy talk.

"Young Mr. Colby dines here frequently," he said, "but I don't know him beyond that." He lowered his gaze. "But, Mike—I'm not comfortable talking about my customers."

"You'd be helping him."

He raised a palm. "You said Mr. Colby was unhappy with you looking into—"

"His father feels otherwise. *I* feel otherwise."

Shaking his head, Pete said, "I still don't see how I can help."

Velda put a hand on his sleeve and said, "Just answer a few questions, Pete. Please. What could it hurt?"

The restaurant owner swallowed. "Well…all right. But I reserve the right to decline to answer."

Velda smiled. "Take the Fifth all you like, Pete."

"So," he said, "what do you want to know?"

"You can tell me," I said, "if your hostess is banging your bartender."

The crudity of that made him blink, but his answer was damn near a non sequitur. "I have several bartenders on staff."

I gave him a narrow-eyed look that was less than friendly. "Not tonight you don't. You know what I'm talking about, Pete. *Who* I'm talking about."

He shrugged. "You mean Gino."

"If that's his name, I do. The dark-haired jamoke working the tap right now."

"Yes. Gino Mazzini. Does a good job. Doesn't cause trouble. Not super-friendly, not a tell-your-troubles-to type bartender, but skilled. Efficient. Not surly."

Not surly. What a commendation.

I said, "So. Is he involved with Sheila?"

Pete shook his head, but that didn't exactly mean no. "You should ask her that."

"Okay. Fair enough. But do you think she *might* be? Hooking up with him?"

After a moment, he nodded.

"Could she be involved with Colby, too? Banging both at the same time?"

Velda frowned at me, then quickly smiled at Pete. "What Mike means, could she be seeing both of them?"

"Right," I said, "I wasn't talking *ménage a twat* or anything."

Velda rolled her eyes.

Pete was shaking his head again. "You'd have to—"

"Ask *her*, right, right. I will. But right now I'm asking you—which of them gave her those shiners?"

His eyebrows rose. "What shiners?"

"Pete…"

He swallowed. We'd been keeping it *sotto voce* already, but now he whispered. "The Mazzini kid did that. They're seeing each other. I think…I think they live together in the Village."

"Which one's worked here the longest?"

"Miss Ryan." He leaned toward me. "Mike, Sheila's been here for four or five years—you know that."

"I guess I do. Where's she from?"

Pete shrugged. "Midwest somewhere. Minnesota, Michigan, Wisconsin, one of those. She came to the city to be an actress and it didn't work out, at least not yet. She's tops, Mike. Everybody loves her."

"Sounds like that includes Colby and Mazzini."

A palm came up. "I don't generally get involved with my employees' private lives."

I ignored that. "What's the story with her and the rich kid? How often does Colby come around to the Chophouse?"

"He's a good customer," Pete said vaguely.

"Did Sheila already know him? Or did they meet here? Was he maybe taken with her? She's an attractive woman."

Velda said, "An understatement."

The restauranteur sighed. "I believe they met here. They became friendly. They sometimes talk. They obviously like each other. They have good, what-do-you-call-it... chemistry."

I said, "What kind of experiments do you think they're conducting?"

Pete shifted in his seat. "Please, Mike. This really makes me uncomfortable. You're asking me to talk trash about two good employees and, if that weren't enough, a customer who spends money like it's paper. You should talk to *them*, not me."

"Excellent idea. How about sending Sheila over?"

He frowned. "She's my hostess, Mike. If somebody comes in…"

"I'll shoo her over. Come on, Pete. I'm a customer, too, you know."

He pulled air in and let it out through as sickly a smile as I'd seen in a while. "Fine, Mike. Anything you say."

Pete slid out of the booth and went over to the hostess podium and spoke a few words, gesturing toward us; Sheila frowned, not a deep frown but a troubled look, and decidedly put-upon. But she came over, striding now, not her usual glide.

She stood before us with her chin up and her eyes down; she might have been a cop who came upon Velda and me playing hide the salami in some Central Park bushes. "Something you wanted, Mr. Hammer?"

I gestured. "You remember my secretary—Velda Sterling?"

"Of course." Sheila nodded. "Ms. Sterling."

Velda nodded back, said, "Ms. Ryan," and I said, "Will you join us for a few moments?"

The hostess's smile was strained. "Could it wait for another time? I *am* working."

"It's not busy, and your boss sent you over. We'll understand if a patron enters and needs your attention. Please."

Like Pete, she chose to slide in on Velda's side.

"Sheila," I said, "I'm working for Vincent Colby's father, looking into the hit-and-run that put his son in the hospital. Where you and I last spoke."

She said nothing.

"The police aren't getting anywhere," I said, "but of course they aren't aware of certain things."

She said nothing.

"I'm hoping you'll be frank with me," I said, "and confirm, or convincingly deny, that you and Colby are seeing each other... behind your *other* boy friend's back. And perhaps you can substantiate that this other boy friend found out about it, and wasn't happy."

She said nothing.

Velda gave it a try, saying, "One of your two admirers gave you that black eye. The second in a couple of weeks. That's quite a collection you're racking up there, Ms. Ryan."

She said nothing.

I asked, "Was it your friend behind the bar?"

Gino's eyes were on us, burning like coals.

She said nothing.

I said, "Or maybe Colby did it. Maybe you're not seeing him, but he's been hounding you, even stalking you, and you confronted him and he lost his head, demanding you break it off with Mazzini. Colby's a regular Jekyll and Hyde these days, thanks to that 'accident.'"

She glared and me and clenched teeth parted only enough for her to get out a few bitter words: "I thought you were smart. You're the famous Mike Hammer, big detective."

"Famous enough," I said with a shrug. "Big enough, too, maybe. But you imply I'm also not smart enough—smart enough for what?"

The words came quick. "Vincent hadn't been hit by that car yet when you saw me with a black eye. These...outbursts of his were caused by that concussion, which hadn't even fucking *happened* yet!"

I grinned. "So you two *are* an item."

Even with her features tightened up in anger, she was a beauty. "I told you before—we're just friends."

"I've seen the way he looks at you, honey, and it's not the way you look at a friend. More like a famished man views a meal."

She huffed a feminine grunt. "Believe what you like."

Velda touched the young woman's arm. "Ms. Ryan, Sheila— please understand. All we're trying to do is help Vincent Colby."

She shook her head, seeming more frustrated than angry. "What does it matter *who* hit Vincent in *what* car? How does *that* help him? He's...he's been hurt...he's...having a terrible time of it. He might have died." She choked back emotion. "All right. All right! I've been seeing him. At first, I...he pressed so hard, he was so insistent, it made me uncomfortable. And I was seeing someone else..."

"Gino," Velda said.

Sheila nodded. "Yes, but Vincent was so attentive, so tender, so…it sounds silly, but…adoring." Her eyes went to Velda, beseechingly. "You probably know what that feels like, Ms. Sterling. You're a lovely woman, a stunning woman. You've had men adore *you*, haven't you?'

I said, "She has one right now."

Sheila actually smiled a little. "I've broken it off with Gino. We're through. He knows that."

Velda said, "*He* gave you that eye."

She nodded. "But I've moved out on him. We were sharing an apartment in the Village. I'm with a girl friend now. Gino is past history. But it's just…tricky. It's hard. To still work where he does."

"Must be," I said.

Velda said, "Here's the thing, Ms. Ryan. We're not just trying to find the hit-and-run driver. We're trying to determine if it was a hired job—if your Gino or someone else in Vincent's life tried to have him killed in what would be written off as an accident."

"That's silly," Sheila said. "I told you—Gino could never afford that. He doesn't have money or friends with money, either."

I said, "On the other hand, Colby works in the world of high finance. He may have enemies in those same rarefied circles. And we don't know yet who in his social circles, which are also pretty damn rarefied, might have a deadly grudge against him. We'll be looking into that."

"Another, larger investigative firm," Velda said, "is exploring the financial world aspects. Someone with Vincent's wealth, his family's fortune and standing, can be a target for all sorts of things, for all sorts of reasons."

The young woman thought about it. Neither Velda nor I pushed her any further. Our case had been made.

Finally Sheila said, "Gino gave me both black eyes. I think you've probably already come to that conclusion yourselves. But it's ridiculous to think he might have hired someone to drive that sports car and try to kill or, what, frighten Vincent off? I hope you're not assuming, because of his last name, that Gino has Mafia connections or any such foolishness. He's like me— he came to New York from a small town to be an actor, and he's still trying to be one, but just like I wound up a waitress, he became a bartender."

Velda asked, "Are you still pursuing acting?"

"Still making a somewhat half-hearted attempt of it, I admit. I audition, just not as frequently…as doggedly. It wears you down after a while."

I said encouragingly, "You're not a waitress. You're a hostess."

She laughed a little. "You sure know how to build up a girl, Mr. Hammer."

Velda was smiling a little. Apparently men can be idiots sometimes. Who knew?

Sheila said, "Before you go, I'll give you my phone number at my girl friend's. I'll help you any way I can. I'll encourage Vincent to cooperate. He isn't always Mr. Hyde. Even now, he's usually Dr. Jekyll."

She got up, smiled and nodded pleasantly. And now when she returned to her post, the hostess in green glided.

"Getting somewhere," I said.

"I feel bad for her," Velda said.

"Why's that?"

"She's gone from an abusive boy friend to another guy with a terrible temper. Of course, that doesn't mean Vincent would strike her or anything, but…it's an unsettling possibility."

I shrugged. "Well, it's helpful to know she's cooperating with us now."

Velda nodded. "It is."

"But I think before this goes any further, I should talk to Casey Shannon, and get the skinny as he sees it where Vincent Colby is concerned. There's a couple of other suspicious deaths on the fringes here."

She touched my hand. "I forgot to tell you, Mike. I spoke to Pat this afternoon, on some follow-up on that Penta case."

"Oh?"

"He said in passing that Shannon has gone to the Keys for a getaway vacation. Will be out of town two or three weeks anyway. There's some old gal friend of his down there he's going to be shacking up with."

I put on a wistful look. "If only I had an old gal friend to shack up with."

"You want to get kicked again?"

We paid at the register and I collected my hat and coat from the blonde near the door. Pete approached and was his old smiling self again.

"Everything work out okay with Sheila?" he asked. "She came away in a good mood, Mike, so you must have behaved yourself."

"Velda's a calming influence."

He was closing up, the place almost empty. Last call here was 1 a.m., and the clock was fifteen minutes fast, as was the custom in so many bars.

We stepped out into crisp autumn air—my favorite time of year. Traffic was light, and we'd have to walk to the nearest corner to grab a cab going in the right direction. I paused to give Velda a quick verbal reconstruction of the hit-and-run, painting the picture as best I could.

"Wouldn't have happened," Velda said, "if he'd parked in that ramp down the block."

"Are you kidding? Rich guys hate to pay."

An unfamiliar hand settled on my shoulder, hard enough to squeeze through the topcoat fabric.

"You better fucking listen," a baritone voice snarled, "you son of a bitch..."

It was the bartender, his breath visible in the chill, coming out his nostrils like dragon's breath.

Gino Mazzini was handsome in a Travolta sort of way, dark-haired, olive-complected with big teeth that looked nasty with that upper lip curled back. "You stay away from my girl—leave her alone! Hear me? Stay the hell away from her, old man, or I'll put you in a damn wheelchair!"

I should have decked him then and there, but I might need to interview him later, and beating him to a pulp might alienate him.

So I said, "Cool it," holding my hands out, palms open. "I'm investigating that hit-and-run and had a few questions for her. That's all. She's in no trouble, and you may have noticed I already have a girl."

I saw it coming, the sucker punch that would have brought

up my steak sandwich, and I bobbed to one side, my hat flying off, but that got me just off-balance enough for him to turn his missed blow into a swinging backhand that knocked me to the sidewalk. Now I was ready to see anything and everything that this prick could send my way, and that included the kick he aimed at my ribs as I lay sprawled on my side. I caught his foot in two hands in midair and yanked it like I was uprooting a small tree and the world went out from under him but obligingly came up to meet him, and the way he landed on cement on his back like that had to hurt like hell. His breath whooshed out like a dam bursting and now, as I got to my feet, it was my turn. I stomped on his stomach with one foot, like he was a big goddamn bug, and then stepped away as he curled up in a fetal ball, hugging himself, his moans stitched together with whimpering.

Somebody in the restaurant must have seen the fun out the tinted-glass windows, because Pete and a few patrons and, of course, Sheila Ryan came bounding out onto the street. Nothing so impressive as a hit-and-run to gawk at this time around, just a scuffle that had ended in pain for the shit who started it.

Only then I got greedy. I leaned in and straddled him and grabbed him by his white shirt and pulled him up to where I could grin into his face.

"Not as easy," I said, getting ready to smack him one more time, "as hitting women, is it?"

But he was younger than me, and for all his pain he managed to swing a fist into my side. The bartender had some power left because it was enough to knock me off him. He was just getting up, ready to come at me again, when his eyes opened wide.

He could feel the snout of the little .32 automatic at his temple.

Velda said through a lovely terrible smile, "Of course with some women, it's not easy at all."

Then she thumped him on the head with the barrel and he went down on his knees, trying not to cry but not making it.

The diminutive Pete was looming over his fallen bartender now. "Your ass is *fired*, you dumb bastard!"

Then the restauranteur came over to apologize as his hostess and the handful of patrons trailed back inside.

"He must not know," Pete said, "who Mike Hammer is."

"I forgot for a minute there myself," I said, smoothing my coat, looking around for my hat.

CHAPTER FIVE

The next morning, behind the door with CAPTAIN PAT CHAMBERS, HOMICIDE DIVISION lettered in gold-outlined black, I was sitting across from my old friend in his painfully modern, glassed-in office at One Police Plaza. I was sipping coffee laced with my usual milk and sugar, my coat and hat hung up with his on a metal tree. We were waiting for a call from a guy he knew on the Accident Investigation Squad.

With his own cup of coffee going, black, Pat was in shirt sleeves and loose tie, and he was scratching at his blond head of hair as he studied me. Cops were wearing their hair way too damn long for my taste these days.

"Mike," Pat said, leaning back in the old anomaly of a brown-leather swivel chair he'd brought over with him from the ancient Centre Street HQ, "you stay up on things. Always seem to know what's going on in your field. Right on top of whatever new tricks the bad guys are up to."

"I try, buddy. Thanks for noticing."

Then came the zinger: "So how is it you're so backward when it comes to making use of modern technology?"

My laugh was short but not sweet. "What are you talking about, Pat? I have a top private forensics lab where I can get things checked out when need be. I have connections with the FBI and CIA and alphabet soup guys you don't even know exist, and all their resources. I consult with top security company experts. And I have an in with a high-ranking cop who gets me access to what I need from *his* lab and other sources. Maybe you saw him in the mirror this morning."

"That's not what I mean."

"What *do* you mean, pal?"

He gestured vaguely toward me with his free hand. "You and that old service model .45 you carry. M1911, referencing the year that antique dates to. The so-called 'Colt Government.' It's big, it's heavy, and you haul it under your shoulder like something out of an old black-and-white movie. Hell, man, why don't you go over to Frielich's and get yourself something state-of-the-art? You can afford it."

For a couple of seconds I just looked at him, then let out a grunt, uncrossed my legs, set the coffee cup on his desk, and sat up.

Then I slipped my hand inside my jacket, under my left arm, and slid the piece free of the holster. I regarded the weapon. The bluing was thinning out, the butts were well-worn, and the edges of the thumb rest were nicked. But it had that satisfying machine-clean oily smell and felt alive in my hand.

"It's like me, man," I said. "An oldie but goodie."

Still leaning back, Pat was grinning as he flipped his jacket back to pat the S & W .38 in the speed rig on his hip.

"Modern technology," he said. "You should give it a try."

"Why?" I tossed him a nasty grin. "Think you could out-draw me, Pat?"

Smirking, he said, "What, you figure this is the Wild West or something?"

"You bet your ass I do. You've been out on these streets. You know how the stats read."

His eyebrows flicked up and he shrugged. "No argument, buddy."

"Anyway, you're forgetting something."

"I am?"

"Sure. The old western gunfighter rule."

His grin reversed itself. "Which is?"

"Don't ever try to out-draw a guy who already has a gun in his hand."

I let him have a look down the big hole at the end of the barrel, watched him as he sucked in a breath, then I chuckled and snugged the gun back in its leather womb.

Pat waited a second before he breathed out and said, "Damn, Mike, the old gunfighters *also* said never draw a gun unless you intend to use it! Man, you're a real pisser—you scare the hell out of me sometimes."

"Just sometimes?"

The phone rang and Pat grabbed the receiver.

The call didn't last long, but most of the talking was on the other end, while Pat leaned forward jotting on a notepad and saying "Uh-huh" now and then, till he thanked his guy and hung up.

He rocked back. "Guess how many red Ferraris there are in the greater New York City metro area."

"I don't know. Twenty?"

"You're close—*three-hundred*-and-twenty. Four-hundred-and-seventeen, state-wide."

I grunted something that was almost a laugh. "More people have dough than I thought. And decent taste."

"Do I have to tell you what that means?"

"Red's a popular color?"

But we both knew what it really meant was that although the case was still in the Active pile, the hit-and-run outside Pete's Chophouse a little over two weeks ago was already a dead issue.

I asked, "Didn't those dicks come up with *anything*?"

He smirked again. "I'm gonna give you the benefit of the doubt that by 'dicks' you mean detectives. They did, actually. Several eyeball witnesses saw that red sports car hauling ass from the scene. Mud-smeared plates, fore and aft. A bearded guy with a pony tail, which is what you saw, right?"

"Right."

"Not enough to identify him."

"Not enough to identify him. Anything else?"

Pat sipped more coffee, nodded; beyond the windowed walls the bullpen murmured with slow-moving but constant activity.

"Yeah, there is," Pat said. "We know the guy turned left on Lex and sideswiped that newsstand on the corner. Paint samples were gathered, so if the right red Ferrari gets itself found, out of those 320 or 417, we'll have our man."

You had to know Pat as well as I did to pick up on the sarcasm in his tone. I felt sure the NYPD would dig into this hit-and-run with a victim out of the hospital the next day—just as soon as they got through tracking down the Star of India that was stolen in 1964.

I wasn't saying anything, because I knew something Pat didn't, or anyway had forgotten. But my silence and my expression were enough to jog his memory.

Eyes narrowing, he said, "That's the newsstand on the corner of Lexington and 44th."

"Is it?"

"That little midget they call Billy Batson, who runs the stand, he witnessed another hit-and-run, what? Twenty years ago?"

"Did he?"

"Kind of a pal of yours, isn't he?"

My shrug maybe tried a little too hard. "I pick up my magazines there. By the way, all midgets are little."

"Thanks a bunch for the intel."

"No trouble."

Pat sighed. "Y'know, Mike—most detectives hate coincidences. *I* hate coincidences. But you seem to thrive on them. Hell, you seem to *attract* them."

"You mind if we change the subject to something besides what a disappointment I am to you?"

"Do I have a choice?"

I leaned forward, set my empty coffee cup on his desk. "Is there a number where Casey Shannon can be reached? You told Velda that he's shacked up with some old honey of his somewhere in the Florida Keys."

Nodding, Pat said, "That's what his last partner, Chris Peters, told me...but Chris also said Casey left specific instructions he didn't want to be bothered."

"Meaning he didn't leave a number. How about an address?"

"Not that I know of." The gray-blue eyes narrowed. "Why?"

I sat back in my chair. "Shannon said he ran into Vincent Colby during the course of two separate suspicious-death inquiries."

"I remember that conversation," Pat said, nodding again. "But he didn't indicate Colby was a person of interest, much less a suspect. I thought you said you were working for his old man—Vance Colby, the Wall Street big shot."

"I am."

"So whose side are you on in this thing?"

"What thing?"

Pat closed his eyes. Then he opened them and said, "Sorry. I should have remembered that you're only interested in truth and justice."

"Don't forget the American way."

"Do I need to remind you what your rich client hired you to do?"

"No."

But he did anyway: "You're looking to find out who was driving that red speed buggy, and bring him in."

"That's the job."

Pat leaned forward. "In other words, Vance Colby has hired you to do what the entire New York Police Department and its considerable resources aren't capable of?"

"Why, how do *you* think they're doing?"

He lifted a forefinger and waggled it at me. "I'm guessing you think that accident was no accident. That it wasn't a hit-and-run, but a hit *period*...one that didn't take."

"I'm looking at that, yeah."

He raised two open hands, as if he were holding them out to catch somebody but didn't care if it worked. "A hit for what reason? I know a lot of people who would like to kill their brokers, but I doubt very many go through with it."

Now I leaned in. "I'm not looking into that side of it, Pat. The old man has specialists in high finance on that score. I'm strictly digging into young Colby's personal life."

Pat shrugged. "Well, I told you—Vincent Colby's clean. I think there may have been some youthful indiscretions, but if so, they've been expunged. That happens under certain circumstances even if you aren't wealthy."

"Which the Colbys certainly are. So, Captain Chambers… should I talk to Chris Peters or do you want to do it?"

Half a smirk settled in a cheek. "To see what Chris knows about those two suspicious deaths somehow tied to our boy Vincent? I can handle that and get back to you. You don't even have to remind me that I work for you, civic-minded tax-payer that you are."

The sky looked as cold and gray as the towers of commerce crowding it, my breath smoking like I hadn't given up Luckies all those years ago. Winter really seemed to be getting ahead of itself and if snow started in, before the leaves were off the trees in Central Park, I was going to be pissed. I had the trenchcoat lining in and a wool suit on, the porkpie squatting on my head keeping my head warm but not the sun out, because there wasn't any. I couldn't quite bring myself to putting on gloves, but you can bet my hands were in my topcoat pockets.

At his newsstand on the corner of Lexington and 44th, Billy Batson was bundled up, too, in his striped red-and-black stocking cap, green plaid woolen scarf, padded quilt jacket, gray flannel trousers, and high-top sneakers. But his cotton gloves had the fingertips cut off so he could handle with ease change and paper money, too.

Like Pat had said, Billy was a midget, but as little people went, this one was on the tall side, and the next time you see *The Wizard of Oz*, see if you can't spot Billy looming above the rest of the Munchkins—no joke, he's there. He'd been one of the famous Singer Midgets before plowing his showbiz dough into this newsstand half a lifetime ago.

Billy's last name wasn't actually Batson, of course—though I had no idea what it really was. Back in the fifties, he'd had the finest newsstand display of comic books on any Manhattan street corner, and still did, though *Spider-Man* and *The X-Men* had long-since banished *Blue Beetle* and *Black Cat*. So it was no surprise that Billy's nickname was Captain Marvel's secret identity, since that's who newsboy Billy Batson in those funny books would turn into after crying out, "Shazam!"

But the Superman people had sued Captain Marvel out of existence in the early fifties, breaking the real-life Billy Batson's heart. Then, not long ago, the company that killed the character revived him themselves, and boy, was Billy proud. He gave those new comic books prime display space and those who knew the significance (sometimes out-of-town comic book collectors who had heard of the real-life Billy Batson) would come by to have him autograph the latest issue of what was now called *Shazam!*

Billy was a wizened little guy these days, even more so than years before, his mug a swirl of wrinkles swallowing up his features; but his eyes were bright and his dentures white, and not much got past him.

"Got the new *Guns & Ammo* and *Ring* for ya, Mike," he said, reaching under his counter for the "pull" mags. "*Playboy*, too. Little lefty for you these days, ain't it?"

"Do I look like I buy it for the articles?"

Those dentures flashed. "Then should I maybe put *Cavalier* back on the list?"

"Naw, it's got a little raunchy for my taste. Anyway, I got better at home."

The bright eyes twinkled. "I'll say ya do! How *is* Velda?"

The modest-sized man had a giant-sized crush on Velda.

"Big and beautiful and mine, Billy," I told him, accepting the magazines and paying him for them. "Don't you get any ideas."

He got my change for me, the bills from his cash register, the coins from the changer at his waist. "You can't stop a guy from havin' ideas, Mike! Say, we got somethin' in common."

"Besides being in love with my secretary?"

"Yeah! I read in the *News* you was a witness to that hit-and-run a few weeks back! Some rich Wall Street guy, huh? Hurt bad, was he?"

I shook my head. "No, he's fine. But that's why I'm here. The cops from the Accident Investigation Squad talked to you?"

His eyes got big. "Yeah. I damn near got hit *myself*, y'know!"

"I didn't know."

He sold a *Times* to a customer, then resumed his tale, gesturing melodramatically. "I was packin' up for the night when that buggy came screamin' around the corner, up and over the curb, sending me divin' for cover, and takin' a piece of my stand with it. Mags knocked all over hell!"

"Show me."

He walked me over. The left side of his stand, just below the display counter, had some rough grooves in it and a chunk of ancient wood was gone, revealing a lighter shade, a fresh wound in its aged hull.

I asked, "Did they hit the headlight, or more like scrape the side of the car?"

"Front right headlight, Mike. And I heard the glass shatter. I told the cops that, but neither one wrote it down. Maybe they got good memories."

"What *did* they do?"

"Took some paint samples," Billy said, then smirked and shook his head dismissively. "But they was half-ass all the way."

"Yeah?"

He sold a *Sports Illustrated* to a guy, then held his hands out, palms up. "I *tried* to tell 'em! They wouldn't listen. You know, I'm *short*, not stupid! That was a *special* Ferrari, Mike, I told 'em it was! But they just made me for some old kook."

I put a hand on his shoulder. "That's not *my* opinion, Billy. What was special about it? There's no shortage of red Ferraris in this town, I'm told."

He was shaking his head before I even finished. "That wasn't just *any* Ferrari, Mike." He waggled a forefinger at me. "I'm *into* sports cars, you know."

That put some wild funny images in my brain, but I didn't let my grin get out of hand. "Really."

"Really."

The little guy sold a *New York* magazine and some Certs to a pretty young woman.

"Yeah," Billy said, rather grandly, "I read damn near *all* the periodicals. News, sports, *People*, *Variety*, you name it. I'm my own best customer! I just never buy anything. I never miss *Car and Driver*, *Motor Trend*, hell, even *Hot Rod*. I told those dumb cops I was a expert! They just laughed and said, 'Sure you are, Pop.'"

Billy had me sold—both that those cops were dumb and that he wasn't, not about cars anyway.

So I asked, "A specific Ferrari how, Billy?"

He wagged a forefinger at me. "That was a F40. Built to satisfy Enzo Ferrari's dyin' wish—ol' Enzo said he wanted to create the best car on planet earth! He took his cue from the 288 GTO—know it? That F40's one fast, powerful ride, my friend. Did you notice the spoiler on the back of that baby, when that guy got clipped?"

"I did," I said, nodding. "Takes away from the sleek look of it. But I could learn to live with that, if somebody gave me one for Christmas."

"Well, without that spoiler, Mike, in a ride with a top cruisin' speed pushing 200 miles per hour like that? It wouldn't be a *bullet* took Mike Hammer out, but metal and fire and asphalt. It's simple aerodynamics, y'know. No spoiler and you could take off like a rocket—goin' straight up! And what goes up, goes you-know-where."

He sold another *Times*.

I put a hand on his shoulder again. "All the years I've known you, Billy, and I never picked up on you being a car buff. What do *you* drive, anyway?"

I figured it would be bad taste to ask him if he had to use blocks for his feet to reach the pedals.

Billy Batson batted the air, made a face, which with that mug was saying something.

"Oh, hell, Mike, I can't drive! Never bothered to learn. What's the point, in the city?"

I took Velda out for lunch at Charlie's Deli. It was one of those gimmick places with lots of '50s nostalgia by way of Elvis on the jukebox, vintage advertising signs on the walls, and gum-snapping waitresses in poodle skirts.

But the food was authentic, even if the atmosphere was ersatz. Velda had a salad with chicken and I chowed down on a pastrami, corned beef and Swiss on rye, coleslaw on the sandwich. Billy might be right that it wouldn't be a bullet that took Mike Hammer out.

I filled her in on my conversation with Pat, and shared what I'd learned from Billy, including that the pride of Singer's Midgets still had a tall yen for her.

"Opinion," I said, between bites.

She shrugged. "I think I'll stick with you, Mike. Billy has a nice business going there, but you may make the grade one of these days."

I tried not to smile and failed. "No. I mean, do I share what Billy told me with Pat?"

"That the Ferrari in question is a special model? Possibly rare?"

"Yeah."

"It's what a good citizen would do."

"So—no, then."

She smiled, spearing a piece of broiled chicken from the salad. "I didn't say that exactly. But you're not wrong. If Pat goes to the Accident Squad clowns who caught the hit-and-run, they might track those leads down...maybe...but who knows what they'll do with it, if they do?"

I sighed deep. "It's been over two weeks. That ride's had its bodywork done on the q.t. by now. Maybe the NYPD's finest will prove it's been worked on, but even so, we're still looking at a hit-and-run with no real description of the driver, no license plate number, and a victim who spent a single night in the hospital."

"Right. Or," she said, and chewed chicken, then swallowed it, and continued, "I can call my contact at Motor Vehicles and ask her to run a check on how many...what's that model called again?"

"An F40."

She shrugged; her silk blouse was pink today and she did a bang-up job filling it. "I could call my friend and see how many red F40 Ferraris are in Manhattan, and the state of New York. I'll also ask if either one has been reported stolen, and then perhaps turned up on the street somewhere, either with some slight damage or no damage at all...because it was repaired before being dumped somewhere to be easily found."

The Platters started singing "Only You," and they could have been talking about Velda.

"I oughta marry you, doll," I said.

"You think?"

The answer was two.

Two red F40 Ferraris in Manhattan, and that constituted every one of them in the state of New York.

CHAPTER SIX

That afternoon I found myself, more than a little unexpectedly, back on the thirty-seventh floor of the Financial District building that housed the offices of Colby, Daltree & Levine. Once again I moved largely unnoticed through the boiler room of cold-calling young brokers basking in that green aquarium luster of computer monitors. The murmur of hard sell pretending to be soft sell followed me as I made my way through.

I took the right toward the row of glassed-in offices of the Yuppies who had climbed up a few rungs; in that central, twice-the-size office for the CEO's son, company president Vincent Colby, the massive desk was unattended. Off to my left was a receptionist, a blonde babe in a red blazer with shoulders wider than mine, her tresses up, her glasses round-framed and big-lensed, the better to see me with.

She was seated at a small dark-wood desk and looking formidable for a girl of maybe twenty-two.

"I'm Mr. Hammer," I said.

A mouth worth looking at, its deep-red lipstick outlined in

black, smiled in a businesslike fashion. "Mr. Owens is expecting you. May I take your coat and hat?"

"Sure."

She did, stowing them in a nearby closet, then returned to her desk and used her phone to say Mr. Hammer was here. She listened, said, "Yes sir," and hung up. Very sweetly she told me, "Just knock and you'll be admitted."

"Should I say Joe sent me?"

She frowned in confusion. "Why would you say that?"

"A joke. Little before your time." Damn. I had to get newer material.

"Knocking will be sufficient," she said, and gestured toward a specific office; her nails were the color of her mouth. Even with a doll like Velda at home, I couldn't help wondering what being twenty years younger for an afternoon would be like.

Off to my right, down the hall of exec VP offices leading to the CEO's, another receptionist was looking my way—the old man's forty-something guardian at the gate, that no-nonsense brunette in the black-framed masculine specs. Snugly curvy in a brown striped power suit, the Ice Queen with the glass-cutter cheeks apparently remembered I'd been a welcome guest yesterday, because she granted me a slight nod and slighter smile.

I grinned and waved at her enthusiastically like a kid from a back seat. It actually made her smile broaden a little and maybe she even stifled a laugh. *You still got it, Hammer,* I thought—if they were over forty, anyway.

The inhabitant of the office labeled WILLIAM J. OWENS, MANAGING DIRECTOR saw me approaching—a blond

Yuppie under thirty in the mandatory shirt sleeves and bright suspenders (dark orange). He was just hanging up his phone, and motioning me in.

I did so.

He was handsome in a Beach Boys Go to College way, hair tousled on purpose and frozen that way with product. His eyes were blue and heavy-lidded, making me think grass not coke was his likely recreational drug of choice; his nose was misshapen as a result of a break or two that indicated he had once been athletic. Maybe he still was. His mouth was small and clenched. If I were a cruder man, I'd say it reminded me of an anus.

"Mr. Hammer," he said, half-rising, extending a hand for me to shake. I did. It was slippery. He gestured for me to sit in the client's chair. I did.

"Appreciate you seeing me, Mr. Owens," I said, "at such short notice."

When he spoke, the little mouth sort of blew a kiss; combined with the other thing that orifice reminded me of, that was disturbing.

He said, "I was intrigued when I heard who it was. Who you *are*. My father used to get a kick out of reading about you in the papers, back when you stirred things up around town."

I just smiled and nodded. Everybody's father seemed impressed with me.

He sat forward, cocked his head and folded his hands; on the low-slung cabinet behind him, a trio of green monitor screens glowed, their cursors pulsing. "What's this about my Ferrari?"

Yes, one of the two F40 Ferraris in Manhattan had turned out to belong to an employee of the Colby brokerage firm—this young exec, in fact.

I had called the other F40 owner, an attorney named Randall with Weiss & Lambrusa, a firm with a pricey Broadway office and a big reputation. The attorney had told me that his vehicle was housed at a private garage and that he'd used it just this past weekend. It hadn't been stolen and he had not noticed signs of damage. I took down the information about where he stowed the wheels, to see if somebody there might have "borrowed" the Ferrari.

But that could wait.

An F40 owner who worked at Colby, Daltree & Levine seemed a more logical priority, and a higher one.

Despite what Captain Chambers had said about my thriving on coincidences, really I was just as wary about them as the next detective. I just didn't view every coincidence as an impossibility or, for that matter, a conspiracy.

After all, this young exec had a high-paying enough job to be one of that elite group of Manhattanites who could afford to own a Ferrari F40.

I had made this appointment by phone through that Red Riding Hood out there. The receptionist had checked with Mr. Owens while I waited on the line; all she had available to pass along were my name and my desire to talk to Owens about his Ferrari. I hadn't expected that paltry info would lead to him getting on to talk to me directly, and was surprised when I got the go-ahead to come around. Right around, if possible.

Which I had.

"Obviously you're aware," I said to my mysteriously cooperative host, "that your associate, Vincent Colby, had a narrow scrape with a hit-and-run recently."

His shrug was a tossed-off thing. "Of course. And I'm relieved, *all* of us are, that Vincent wasn't badly hurt, although…well, we're all relieved."

I put an ankle on a knee. "If you were about to say that you're concerned about the aftereffects of his concussion, that's no surprise to me. I'm working for Vincent's father, looking into the 'accident.'"

The tiny mouth tightened. "Yes…I know."

I frowned. "Vance Colby *told* you?"

Owens widened his eyes but they didn't lose their sleepy look. "Well…I work closely with Vincent. He's more the big-picture guy around here. I'm essentially the office manager. We're friends since college. Not a lot of secrets."

"So you know about his fits of temper."

His laugh was abrupt, cutting itself off. "Recent days, I've been on the wrong end of them, yes, a few times. And let me tell you, Mr. Hammer, this is something very new, and most disturbing. I've known some cool cats in my time, but few cats are as cool, and collected, as Vincent."

"That's the impression I got from his father. Losing that cool of his seems out of character for Vincent Colby."

The blond broker squinted at me, as if trying to bring me into focus. "So what's the connection here between Vincent's hit-and-run and my Ferrari? You can't be implying that it was *my* car that gave him that narrow escape. My F40 is in the shop and *has* been for a good month."

That didn't mean someone else couldn't have used it.

But I kept that thought to myself and instead asked, "Did Vincent mention to you that a red Ferrari was the vehicle in question?"

Frowning, nodding, Owens said, "He did, actually. He…he even kidded me about it. 'Where were you at the night of November whatever-it-was?' But, Mr. Hammer, there must be a *hundred* red Ferraris in New York!"

"Actually, four hundred and seventeen."

His head rocked back a little. "Wow. Well, I admit I'm surprised. I thought I was in rather select company."

"You are. There are only two F40s in Manhattan."

His eyebrows went up; they were so blond, they were barely there. "Oh. Well. I can see why you're here, then."

"Would Vincent be familiar with your car? Has he ridden in it?"

With a slow, thoughtful shake of his head, Owens said, "No. Not that I can think of…no, never."

"You said a few moments ago you're friends."

Now he nodded, giving it a little more than was necessary. "We are. But we work together. Rarely socialize these days. And when we do, it's in the city. The only time I drive that car in town is when I'm heading out into the country. And Vincent *hates* the country."

"So he wouldn't have recognized the F40, even if he'd seen it coming."

His eyes tightened as he thought about that, or pretended to.

"I don't know that he's ever *seen* it," Owens said, "but he's heard me *talk* about it enough. The way a proud father talks about his kid, I suppose. I don't *have* any…kids I mean. Mr. Hammer, that vehicle is being worked on. It's a fantastic machine in many ways, but the brakes are frankly shitty."

Some proud father.

He went on: "The rotors and calipers, too, aren't what you'd expect from something so high-end. I've had to have a frustrating amount of maintenance done on it. But I have a top guy who does the work for me."

"High-maintenance ride, huh?"

"Afraid so, but worth it." He grinned puckishly. "Like some females—worth the misery."

I gave that more of a smile than it had coming. "It's in your mechanic's possession now?"

"It is. His name is Roger Kraft." He reached for a notepad and pen, started scribbling. "I'll give you the address."

He tore off the slip of paper and passed it to me across the desk.

"I appreciate this, Mr. Owens," I said, pocketing it. "What does Kraft look like, by the way?"

"Look like? Well, he's about forty. Your size, a little heavier."

"Pony tail? Beard?"

"Heavens no. Neither! Not Roger. He's an ex-Marine." That pinched mouth managed a grin. "He would gladly pummel *any* man who wore a pony tail."

"If that ever comes up," I said, "I'll know who to ask."

I thanked him and stood.

He got to his feet as well and said, "I can't imagine how or why my F40 could have been used in that despicable way. But on the very long shot that it *was*, Mr. Hammer, would you please let me know?"

"You'll be the first," I said.

I was barely out the door when the Ice Queen guarding Vance Colby's gate called out, "Mr. Hammer! A moment please!"

I walked down to her desk. She'd pretty well melted by now, and seemed downright pleasant, saying, "If it's at all convenient, Mr. Colby would like a few words."

"Any particular ones?"

That got a real smile out of her. Every secretary and receptionist in town loved me now.

She said, "You can go right in."

I did.

Vance Colby was seated on one of the facing couches near the fireplace again, flames going full-throttle. People his age get cold easy—really cold when they stop breathing.

"Please join me, Mr. Hammer."

I went over and did that, sitting opposite him. He had a snifter of brandy waiting. We'd graduated from coffee. He poured me a glass and I accepted it. Tasted fine, although what does a beer guy know about brandy?

The plump little man with the trim mustache, wrapped up in another well-tailored pinstripe, poured himself some brandy but set the glass down.

"I am surprised to see you back at Colby so soon," my client said. "Have you something to report?"

I hadn't come to report at all, of course, but he did have ten grand's worth of my time.

So I said, "Just an interesting wrinkle or two."

I told him that I'd confirmed the NYPD was not exactly setting up roadblocks to nab the hit-and-runner; his assumption that they were blowing off the incident would seem to be right on. I also let him know that a specific, rare model of Ferrari had been the vehicle.

Then I informed him of the Ferrari F40 whose owner was parked down the hall.

"You'll most likely find," the old man said, unimpressed, "that's merely a coincidence."

Everybody today was telling me what to think about coincidences.

"William Owens is a good boy," he said, as if I'd suggested otherwise. "He and Vincent were at Harvard together. Met on the rugby team. They think the world of each other. Those two are the future of this firm."

"Well, it's an odd turn of events," I said, then sipped the sweet stuff he'd poured me. "I'll have to look into it."

The faded blue eyes popped. "By all means! I just...when I heard you were on the premises, I assumed you must have come to see me. To bring me up to speed."

"If that Ferrari had been up to speed," I said, "I doubt your son would be alive. Those babies do nearly 200 miles per hour."

"Disturbing. Disturbing."

I nodded toward the door. "Where is your son, by the way? I notice he isn't in his office."

"Psychiatrist. Every day, for now at least. He had a bad one last night. Blew up at me again."

"What set him off?"

He flipped a hand. "I suggested he take a leave of absence. Just for a few weeks or at most months...until his psychiatrist and physician give him a clean bill of health."

Clean bill of *mental* health.

I finished my brandy. Stood. "Thank you, Mr. Colby. I'm glad to have a chance to touch bases with you…but these are early days."

He stood, frowning a little. "*Will* this take days?"

"Figure of speech. But it could take days, yes. My advice is put this out of your mind. Help your son as best you can, and meanwhile I'll find that Ferrari and its driver for you."

A smile blossomed under the skimpy mustache. "You do that, Mr. Hammer, and there will be a handsome bonus in it for you!"

"And I'll accept it."

We shook hands and I went out.

The brunette with the mannish glasses gave me a smile as I passed, nothing icy about her now, though she still had a certain regal air.

But I already had a good-looking brunette in my life for a secretary. And being greedy only got a guy in trouble.

Lower Manhattan was home to plenty of desolate, half-dead business districts like this, rife with crumbling, neglected buildings waiting for gentrification to catch up with them, the street-level storefronts housing dingy shops dealing in junk, out-of-date crap or surplus goods.

I'd been to this particular stretch of small business purgatory before, just a few months ago. The tire-recapping place continued to ooze its bouquet of Butyl rubber into the atmosphere, an open-back truck piled with used casings parked out front, unattended. The tool-and-die shop still wore a CLOSED sign that could mean for the moment but more likely forever, the plate-glass shop had somehow managed to stay above water, and that tune-up and auto repair garage that had just opened for business on my last visit remained a beacon of optimism among a graveyard of empty storefronts.

What the hell would a Ferrari F40 be doing down here?

The wind fluttered the bottom of my trenchcoat and my hat needed to be well-snugged or it would fly away on me. I'd parked half a block down from the address I was checking out—I didn't care to leave my heap too far away, not being as trusting as the tire-recapping boys.

The building on the corner had once been a gas station, probably dating back to the days when the term "service station" was still in use and guys in crisp uniforms and caps came running out to clean your windshields and check your tires, water, battery, oil. That was in the days when the idea of filling your own tank seemed absurd. What were we, farmers? Now the structure was a ghost of that curved '50s architecture that said the future was here—well, it was…a future with its windows painted out, black, giving no view onto the space where once you paid for your gas with cash more often than credit card, and bought candy bars and chewing gum before helping yourself to free road maps.

One of those blacked-out windows had white lettering saying KRAFT AUTOMOTIVE—APPT. ONLY with a phone number. I tried the door and found it unlocked. Just barely ajar. Cracked it further, hollered, "Hello!" and got no response. I pushed it open and stepped inside.

No counter remained in a gutted sales area that was now an office with a metal desk, several filing cabinets and old shelves used to stack automotive catalogues and instruction manuals where cans of oil and other supplies had once lined up like military. Closed doors at left and right still said MEN and WOMEN.

I moved into what had once been the service area, and still was to some degree, with two car lifts, workbenches along the walls, tools on pegboards and the smell of oil. But the garage was clean, almost surgically so, cement floor included. Behind the lifts, and in front of the back workbench, a black full-car cover shrouded a shape that, with the distinctive half-showing star-shaped hubcaps, told a story.

I pulled off the car cover and the red Ferrari said hello. My mouth dropped. I was looking at the fastest, most powerful, and for that matter most expensive car Ferrari ever made.

I checked the passenger side of the vehicle for signs of exterior damage, but there were none. I'd driven stock cars in my reckless youth, but sports cars were out of my league, and that midget with the newsstand knew a hell of a lot more about them than I did. Still, my eyes told me that maybe—maybe—some bodywork had been done around the front right headlight.

Back in the office, I did what any self-respecting private detective would do in a place of interest whose front door was left unlocked. I snooped, starting with the filing cabinets, which held old invoices in their upper drawers and nothing in the lower ones.

On to the desk.

There, the usual business junk shared space with a few surprises, like the .38 Police Special in the right-hand drawer, and a box of ammo in the drawer beneath. Well, a small businessman had the right to protect himself, didn't he? Of more interest, and much more suggestive, were three items in the bottom left drawer—the only items in that drawer.

A false dark-brown beard. A small bottle of yellow liquid labeled "Spirit Gum." A dark long-haired wig with a pony tail.

I shut the drawer, glanced around. Only two places left to check. The MEN was unoccupied. The same couldn't be said for the WOMEN.

A male figure, slumped, hunched over with head hanging, was seated on the toilet, its lid down, his pants up. Even sitting, he was obviously a big man, easily as big as me, burly not fat. His head was shaved. Arms hung limp. Feet, in rubber-soled work boots, were askew. He wore the navy-blue coveralls of the mechanic he was. Or had been.

Carefully, using his ears, I used both hands to lift his head back. His eyes were open and rolled back and filmed-over, dull with death; his tongue-lolling mouth was open, as if seeking breath or sustenance or perhaps an ability to speak, all of which would be forever denied to him. His face was blue with need of a shave, which would be up to his mortician now.

None of that was what was the most disturbing thing. That distinction was left to his upper torso, which was caved in so deep that the top half of his jumpsuit was puckered. He might have taken a cannonball to his chest cavity.

I took a look at the floor leading into the WOMEN and could see the trail of dark rubber from his heels as he'd been dragged, already dead, into the cubicle. In this black-windowed room, next to this desk, someone had somehow shoved this man's chest in.

* * *

A squad car preceded Pat Chambers only by a few minutes. I gave the pair of blues the basics, but waited for Pat to give out chapter and verse. He went around taking it all in, from the dead mechanic in the WOMEN's room to the Ferrari, the black cover to which I had not replaced.

"Sorry about my prints," I said.

We were standing outside now. The crime scene guys were in there shooting their pictures and collecting their evidence. We were just two guys who had both quit cigarettes a long time ago whose breath was smoking in the cold nonetheless.

He shrugged. "You had no way to know."

His unmarked Chevy Caprice was parked on the cement apron of the place where three gas pumps had once sprouted. His radio on the dash squawked for his attention. He went over to it, climbed in, grabbed the mike and, sitting there with the car door open, listened and talked a while. I rocked on my heels and waited. Pat had called R & I to run Roger Kraft through and this appeared to be the callback.

He strolled over. Like me, he was in a trenchcoat and hat. Mine cost more. We taxpayers are stingy bastards, except where we're concerned.

"Roger Kraft has a record," Pat said. "Armed robbery down south. Series of smash-and-grabs at…you'll love this…gas stations. Long time ago. After that he was in the service, motor pool guy."

"Working for Ernie Bilko probably," I said.

"He owned this shop," Pat said, nodding behind us. "But I don't think he went straight. Robbery Division suspects him of being the driver for a crew that's been hitting small banks upstate."

"And now he's gone," I said, "and mankind will just have to bear up."

"You ever see anything like that?"

"The Ferrari F40? Just when it clipped Vincent Colby."

"No. I mean the way that guy died. His fucking chest is sunk in like Popeye punched him."

"A fist didn't do that, even with spinach. Two fists didn't do it, either. I got no idea what did, unless the killer had a battering ram in his pocket."

I'd already filled Pat in about Owens at the Colby brokerage. He'd said nothing then but the back of his mind must've been working on it.

He said, "You think this Owens character hired Kraft to kill his friend?"

"I think Owens hired Kraft to fine-tune his car. And I think if somebody *did* hire this guy to kill the Colby kid, they took advantage of how little Owens used the vehicle to borrow it for the job. Unless Kraft was just out joy-riding."

"Just a coincidence that the Owens vehicle was what he was working on."

"I didn't say that. Come on, Pat—you know how us detectives hate coincidence. There *could* be a connection. Somebody might have recommended Kraft to Owens. I mean, this isn't a part of the city Yuppies generally hang out in. How would William J. Owens stumble onto this place?"

"The Yellow Pages maybe?"

"I doubt Kraft was even *in* the Yellow Pages. This looks like a sub rosa operation."

"Not big enough to be a chop shop."

I frowned. "No, but if Kraft had a reputation for doing good work on high-end rides like the F40, he might get access to machines that could *really* go, for use with that bank-heist crew you mentioned. You need to talk to your contacts in Robbery and see if the M.O. includes getaway cars with impressive pedigrees."

Pat was nodding. "Sometimes you think like a detective."

"You cops ought to try it."

Pat's radio squawked again. More talk, more listening. When he clicked off and returned the handset to its slot, he made a note in his pad and then came over, his expression grim.

He planted himself in front of me and said, "You're not going to like this."

"Tell me anyway."

"Seems something didn't smell good inside Casey Shannon's apartment. The super called it in and our guys broke in and found Shannon there."

"Not in Florida," I said. "Not shacked up with an old honey."

"No. Dead on the floor for a week, anyway. And here's the part you really won't like."

"I already don't like it."

"I know. But get this—somebody caved his chest in."

CHAPTER SEVEN

Tudor City, between Grand Central and the United Nations, was an island of apartment buildings within the island of Manhattan. In the heart of midtown, the cluster of apartments had everything—two lovely parks, great shopping, swell dining. Also the rent-controlled one-bedroom apartment where Lt. Casey Shannon had lived for twenty years, ever since his wife divorced him and he'd moved here from Queens.

The apartment had everything, too—hardwood floors, a separate foyer, a good-size living room, a full kitchen, a bathroom with windows (on the quiet north side of the building) and its one bedroom was damn near as big as the living room. One of a hundred-and-fifty apartments in a building built in 1929 (before the Crash), with a doorman and a laundry room, these digs had it all.

Everything but a living occupant.

Shannon was sitting on the floor with his head slumped, his back against the couch that had stopped his fall. He was in white blue-flecked pajamas under a maroon robe and wearing slippers; his chest looked sunken, a terrible blow of some kind having created a crater that sucked in the fabric of its garments, twisting the cloth like the striations of a spent bullet.

A big damn spent bullet.

But there was no firearm involved in this homicide. And for that ghastly indentation to have been the work of a fist, or even two fists, it would require an Andre-the-Giant-size killer.

When Pat, hat in hand, looming over the grisly corpse, said quietly, "Shit," it was more like a prayer than a curse.

The windows were already up, to air out the smell of death, the job not yet done.

I said, "I didn't know Casey as well as you, buddy. I mostly go back to when he was working with you ten, fifteen years ago. But I knew him enough to know he was a hell of a cop."

"The best." Pat gave me a hard look. "This one's mine, Mike."

"The case you mean? Or the kill?"

"Both."

I shook my head. "No promises, pal. If I get my hands on who did this, I'll take him out. You know I will."

The gray-blue eyes were ice cold. "I'm asking you a favor on this one, Mike. This time it's *my* friend some son of a bitch slaughtered. This is *my* Jack Williams."

Jack had stepped in front of a Jap bayonet and it cost him an arm but saved my ass. Back here at home in the glorious post-war world, a cold-blooded murderer cut Jack down. And I had taken my revenge by way of delivering a slug in the killer's belly, just the way Jack got it. It hadn't been pretty and I still revisited it in my nightmares, but I could do it again. Easily.

"I'll try, Pat. If I get there before you, I'll save the bastard for you. But you're not me. You don't have the stomach for it that I do."

"Oh, I won't kill who did this," he said. "With the death penalty gone, what I want is to watch him squirm in court, suffer public shame and humiliation, his every evil act dragged out and shoved in his face, then spend the rest of his sorry life behind bars, being some animal's bitch."

I shrugged. "To each his own."

We had the place to ourselves for the moment. Two uniforms were in the hall on the door and the forensics team wasn't there yet. I prowled the place, like I was walking point in the jungle.

It was in some ways a typical bachelor pad. Lots of guys are slobs and live in a mess of a place where a woman's touch would have made it habitable. Casey was a thorough and meticulous cop and that had been the way he lived. This pad was neat as the proverbial pin, and whether he vacuumed and dusted himself or had a cleaning woman in, the result was a glimpse into the orderly mind of a top-notch investigator.

A Yuppie with a little dough would have salivated at the very thought of getting this place at twice the rent Shannon had been paying. Their interior decoration would have been far different, however—Casey had clearly furnished the place when he moved in a couple decades ago, raiding the showroom at J.C. Penney or Sears. The pictures on the walls were infrequent and were either hunting scenes or photos of his two grown children and four grandchildren. President Reagan's picture beamed over a vintage wooden file cabinet.

This was a living room that got lived in, or it had been before the murder—TV with lounger opposite, a bookcase with bestsellers (*The Fountainhead*, *Something of Value*, *Anatomy of a Murder*), an old scarred-up desk consuming one corner. His phone was on it and a blotter, and a row of reference books; but no stacked papers or files or anything. I knelt for a look at the three desk drawers. No sign that any one of them had been pried open.

Pat was checking out the kitchen and I was tempted to go through that desk and those drawers, using a handkerchief so as not to leave prints; but that search was rightly Pat's bailiwick—him and the lab boys.

He returned and I met him at the corpse.

"So," I said, "how do you read this?"

His hat was on now, pushed back. "No sign of a struggle. No sign anything's been gone through. Somebody wanted Casey dead. Simple as that."

"Simple," I said. "Some fucker just rolled his civil war cannon in and lit the fuse and aimed at your friend's chest."

He ignored that. "Casey knew the killer. A friend, maybe. Or at least an acquaintance."

"Not necessarily."

"Oh?"

"You can rule out a stranger, because Shannon let the person in, obviously at night, and they ended up across the room. So they spoke a while. I don't think the killer was here long—no coffee cups or beer bottles in the kitchen?"

"None."

I shrugged. "But that doesn't rule out somebody he knew from a case he was working. Somebody who stopped by and said he had some info for Casey and got invited in."

Pat twitched a frown. "And did *that* to him, somehow."

"Yeah."

"But Casey was *retired*."

"Casey was still looking into something having to do with Vincent Colby. For some reason, that was the case that was eating at him enough that he couldn't let it go. Couldn't hang it up till he resolved the damn thing to his investigative mind's satisfaction."

Almost to himself, Pat said, "Every cop has one of those cases."

I walked in a small circle, my hands in the air. "But what *was* it? Vincent Colby's the common denominator, but appears to just have been on the periphery of those things."

"'Those things,' Mike, are called homicide investigations. And, judging by what little I know, both of those deaths are tied to Colby, Daltree & Levine." He waggled a finger at me. "I don't know the details, but I will very damn soon, my friend, that I promise you."

Right on cue, Chris Peters burst in, tramping through the entryway, the badge he'd used to get past the two cops at the door still in hand.

"I heard the call in my car," he said, breathless. The slim blond detective, who'd been Shannon's last partner, reminded me of the young Patrick Chambers. His eyes went white all around. "Jesus! Will you look at him."

He almost ran to his fallen colleague, then stopped short, the cop in him not wanting to disturb anything. Then he dropped to his knees, as if at a shrine.

Swallowing hard, he said, "What happened to him?"

"I don't know," Pat admitted, putting a hand on the detective's shoulder. "Somehow someone crushed his chest in. The M.E. can tell us more, after the autopsy."

Then the young man hung his head, mirroring the corpse nearby. They might have been praying together, but only one of them was crying, the other way past that.

Pat let this go on a while, then helped the boy to his feet. "We'll find who did this. He'll pay."

"He or she," I reminded them. "There's always those two possibilities."

I knew that too well.

Pat walked Shannon's heartsick partner away from the body and positioned the young man and himself so that their backs were to the grim tableau. I came along.

Pat told him, "Mike is working the Colby hit-and-run."

I said, "I'm working for the father's client. Old man Vance Colby."

Of course, Chris had been there that night.

"Well," Peters said, "that whole hit-run thing threw Casey for a curve."

"How so?"

His expression grew thoughtful. "He was at least a little suspicious of Colby's role in those two other homicides. One was a low-level broker at the Colby firm, the other a secretary there."

"Vincent Colby's secretary?"

"No, not exactly. He doesn't have a secretary, even though he's all but running the place. They have a secretarial pool. But the young woman had been in frequent contact with him, taking dictation and such."

As good-looking as the women at that firm seemed to be, I wondered exactly what kind of dictation she'd taken.

"Attractive girl?" I asked.

"Very. Tragic circumstances. She was found raped and strangled in her apartment. Her roommate was away for the weekend and found the body when she got back late on a Sunday night."

Just the kind of thing that could get its claws into a detective, even one who'd seen everything—like Casey Shannon.

I said, "If I'm remembering right, the other homicide was also a hit-and-run."

Peters nodded. "Yes. Different circumstances. The young employee was in the ramp of a parking garage where he kept his own car when he was struck down. No witnesses. Casey thought that one stunk."

My laugh was short and harsh. "I can see why. That reads more as a murder than an accident—you don't work up that kind of speed in a parking ramp unless you're homicidal in one way or another."

Pat said to Peters, "Remind me when these homicides went down."

"The secretary over a year ago," he said. "The other one a good two years ago. But now we have two hit-and-run incidents at the Colby firm, and Vincent is at least a peripheral figure on the two earlier homicides, and the target of the more recent one."

I asked, "Have you been working with Casey on this?"

He shook his head. "Not since he retired. I'm partnered up with another guy and up to my ass in the usual alligators. And even before that, I was encouraging Casey to let the Colby thing drop. We weren't getting anywhere and we had bigger fish to fry. Other fish, anyway. No shortage of homicides in Manhattan."

"No shortage," Pat sighed.

I asked, "Why would he tell you he was going to Florida when he was sticking around to, what? Keep digging?"

"You got me," Peters said, throwing his hands up. "His message came in at work when I was out, so I didn't question him about it."

Pat said, "He knew you didn't agree with him keeping at this thing."

Peters was shaking his head hard, now, exasperated. "But we're at three homicides now, and an apparent attempted murder, all tied to that same brokerage? *Something's* going on."

"Four homicides," I said, and told him about the Kraft kill, and its identical kill MO.

The young detective listened intently, a haunted blankness gradually curdling into something else, his handsome face getting ugly; and he looked like he might start crying again. I couldn't blame him.

Trembling with rage and sorrow, he said, "I want a piece of this, Captain Chambers."

Pat put a hand on the young man's shoulder. "I understand. But you're too personally involved with this one. I'm taking charge of this myself. Of course, I'll need you to be available to me. I want to know everything you've got on those first two homicides."

"Whatever you need, Captain."

"Good. And I'll keep you in the loop."

"Thank you, sir. Thank you."

Pat shooed him off and, after a pathetic look back at his dead partner, Detective Chris Peters left the crime scene.

"What a hypocrite you are," I said, but I was smiling.

"What the hell do you mean?"

"*He's* too personally involved with this one? What are *you*, Pat? Aren't you the guy salivating over killing the killer's chances whenever a parole hearing comes up? Crushing the bastard's dreams of a life beyond prison walls?"

That made him laugh.

I was glad he hadn't lost his sense of humor.

The Tube was one of those well-known nightspots that I'd never had a desire to frequent. That was based on what I'd read and heard. Fact was, I'd never been there at all.

On Twelfth Avenue in Chelsea, the notorious club was housed in a warehouse that was part of a onetime railroad freight terminal. The place was massive, something like eighty-thousand square feet. Train tracks from the turn of the century still ran through a sunken section of what was now a long, narrow dance floor. Railroad sidings from the Eleventh Avenue freight line of the New York Central Railroad once ran directly into the warehouses around here, transferring goods to and from freight cars ferried on barges across the Hudson from Hoboken.

Where workmen had once toiled mightily, young New Yorkers now partied with abandon. Flashing lights bounced off metal tubing along the ceiling and off iron pillars rising from old wood floors within sandblasted brick walls. New Wave and other contemporary music, courtesy of a DJ, blasted at decibel levels unknown to man from massive speakers mounted everywhere.

I moved through alone, a figure out of another era in a hat and trenchcoat, surrounded by an under-forty crowd whose clothing above the waist was loud and expensive and angularly cut, with jeans below, sometimes fashionably torn, other times crisply designer.

I had thought about bringing Velda along, and she might have got a kick out of the place. She had more interest in changing times and new fashions than me, to say the least. But she might have wanted to hang around and take it all in, whereas my intention was to get in and out. Kind of like the couple screwing in a booth near the door to a unisex bathroom. What was becoming of this generation? Didn't they have enough dignity to go into that john and have at it?

I had been led here by Vance Colby, having called my client to say I needed to talk with his son, who I understood still lived with him. Like the late Casey Shannon, the elder Colby had a co-op, but his was on Fifth Avenue with a mere twenty rooms or so, none of which held his son, at the moment—Vincent was out for the evening with a lady friend, and the likeliest place to find him was the Tube. So I'd given it a try.

But with the strobing lights in this dark industrial tunnel-like space with its packed dance floor—with three stories of open wrought-iron walkways looming on either side, other patrons hanging over the railings with drinks and joints in hand—I was having no luck spotting my client's son.

The bar was a squared-off sheet-metal oasis in the middle that I managed to reach and was able to order a rye and ginger from a girl with spiky green hair, a face powdered white and very red lipstick. Her breasts spilled out of the top of her black-and-red bustier like cantaloupes from the back of a produce truck. These kids today.

"Are you Mike Hammer?" a voice said, which clearly had come to

terms with a way to be heard over the deafening crap that Velda had told me as was called techno music.

I turned and the guy standing there was handsome in a sharp-featured way, in a gray sports jacket that probably cost a grand and a white t-shirt that cost a couple bucks and dock pants that cost who gives a shit, an ensemble set off by a black eye-patch that screamed for a parrot on his shoulder.

"Parker Beigen," I said, not quite yelling. "I read about you in the papers. Congratulations on your success."

"I read about you in the papers, too…as a kid!"

Hadn't everybody? Me and Flash Gordon.

"Word of advice?" I said.

"Sure!"

I nodded toward the couple sitting a few squared-off metal stools down from me who were sharing a coke-lined mirror, employing a use for a hundred-dollar bill that I'd never tried.

He grinned. He winked with the visible eye. "You disapprove!"

"I don't give a damn what people do," I said, though that wasn't entirely true. At the old Club 52 I had once flushed a pile of coke down the john and got criticized for it. I was more a live-and-let-live guy now.

He seemed amused, his smile as wry as my drink. "Then what's the problem, Mike? If I may?"

"You may. It's just too wide open. It'll catch up with you."

He shrugged. "I pay handsomely for the privilege."

"Someday you'll run into an honest copper or an administration less corrupt than most, and you'll be finished. A little friendly advice from an old soldier."

"Appreciated." He gestured grandly. "I just don't like to rain on people's parades."

"I hear you. Look, I'm trying to find Vincent Colby."

He frowned just a little.

I said, "Not to bother him. He's in no trouble. I work for his old man. Consider me a friend of the family."

The techno crapola stopped and a song I recognized came on—"Heart of Glass," Blondie. Kind of liked that one, besides which the singer was a foxy little thing. But that song was an oldie, for this place anyway. Like me.

My host said, "Well, Vincent's here. Out on the dance floor somewhere, I'd expect. I could probably find him for you…unless he's up in the Dungeon. That's his favorite of our special rooms, and I'd hate to bother him."

The fabled S & M Room. Every boy needs a hobby.

I said, "I'd appreciate you trying."

He patted me on the back. "Listen, Mike. You're welcome here any time. I don't believe those crazy rumors about you flushing a fortune in coke down the drain."

"Yeah! You're right not to believe everything you hear. But why do you want *my* business?"

He grinned big. "I don't want your business. I want your presence." Another wink. "I'll put you on the list."

"Most of the lists I'm on start with the letter 's.' What's this one about?"

"It's about you not paying for drinks or food or any damn thing under this roof, including a cover charge. Celebrities are what keep this place going."

"I haven't been a celebrity in a long time."

"Sure you are! You have great camp value!"

I had a feeling he wasn't talking about me being an Eagle Scout back in Brooklyn.

He patted my shoulder. "Don't worry, I'll find Vincent for you!"

He headed into the crowd and turned colors with the flashing lights. When people saw him, the way parted like the Red Sea for Moses. Then the Blue Sea, then the Green Sea...

Within two minutes, Vincent Colby and Sheila Ryan, hand in hand, emerged from the frantic crush of dancers and stood before me where I sat at the bar. Like I was the principal and this was my office.

The couple was indistinguishable from the other revelers— wild tops, blue jeans, him in Reeboks, her in Mary Janes.

"Vincent," I said with a nod. "Ms. Ryan."

The curvy redhead nodded back, but her date looked a little sick.

"Mr. Hammer," Vincent said, also skilled at working his words above the noise. He seemed embarrassed. "I'm afraid I was rude to you the other day. I hope we can start over."

"Sure. Is there anywhere in this place where we can talk without yelling?"

He gestured toward the front. "Just step outside, maybe. That work for you?"

"It does."

I downed the rest of my drink and followed them as they moved between the dance floor and the booths.

Not many people were milling out front; it was just a sidewalk along a city street, and cold. Our breaths steamed.

Vincent slipped his arm around Sheila's shoulder, who placed a hand on his chest—Gino who?

I said, "Casey Shannon was murdered."

"What?" Agape, he said, "My God, what happened?"

I filled him in, including the crushed chest cavity, and told him about the similar fate that had met Roger Kraft, the mechanic used by his friend and co-worker, William Owens, on a certain Ferrari—the one that had been tentatively identified as the vehicle in the hit-and-run at Pete's Chophouse.

Sheila looked stricken and Vincent didn't look much better.

"This is a nightmare," he said quietly. "A freaking nightmare."

"We're now at four homicides and your near-miss hit-and-run," I said. "All connected in some fashion to the Colby brokerage… and, frankly, you."

Alarmed, divining the accusation in that, Sheila said, "Mr. Hammer, Vincent and I have been together *all day*!"

I said to him, "I thought you had an appointment with your shrink."

"With my psychiatrist's blessing," Vincent said, "I took a day off from work *and* from therapy. We went to the theater, a matinee, *Cabaret*, ate at the Four Seasons, spent some time at Sheila's apartment, and came here to round the day out with a little harmless fun."

"In the Dungeon Room?"

Sheila blushed, but all Vincent did was smile a little, saying, "It's perfectly innocent, Mr. Hammer. Some mild spanking, whips that don't hurt, hands tied behind the back while your partner does whatever he or she would like, within reason…"

I wondered what "within reason" was in a club where you could get your ashes hauled in a booth and then share a mirror of cocaine with your sweetie-pie.

I asked, "How well did you know Lt. Shannon?"

"We were friendly," Vincent said with a shrug. "At least… superficially. I suspect that *he* suspected *me.*"

"In that secretary's death?"

"Yes. I'd…well, I'd seen Victoria a few times. That was her name, Victoria Dorn. As I say, she and I'd gone out. I'd stayed over a few times." He glanced at Sheila. "Sorry, honey. That was *way* before us." To me he added, "But the lieutenant never found anything, 'cause there was nothing to find."

"What about the other death?"

"Paul Matthews? He was just a broker out on the floor. I didn't know him well. But that was an accident."

I grunted a laugh. "What, like your 'accident' outside Pete's? Vincent—it's no accident when a car has worked up enough speed in a parking ramp to run somebody down."

"That's not true, Mr. Hammer! Think about it—we've all seen people come roaring around corners in parking garages, and said, 'That's guy's crazy!' Maybe not often, but it happens."

He wasn't wrong.

"Look," he said, and swallowed, "I'm getting scared. I don't mind admitting it. Somebody's killing people, and if it wasn't for me being a target myself, I'd say whoever it is, is trying to lay blame on me!"

"Frame you," I said.

He nodded. "It sure feels like it. Sure looks like it."

"I thought you wanted me to stay out of this."

He shook his head slowly. "I was wrong, Mr. Hammer. I was way out of line at Dad's office. I'm trying to work on this, this… *temper* of mine, flaring up like it does. I really can't control it yet. I *am* getting help. You know that."

Sheila hugged his arm. "He's trying. He really is."

"I gather that," I said.

His chin went up slightly. "Mr. Hammer, I want your help. I *need* your help. And I'll cooperate in any way I can."

"You can start by telling me whether you think Shannon was still zeroing in on you."

A sigh. "I can't really say. We were friendly at the gym. But you know, I felt he got a membership there just to…watch me. Get close to me. I got a 'Columbo' vibe off him. You know, he'd spot me when I was working on a machine or lifting weights. Helpful, interested. Just too damn nice."

"It does appear," I said, "that he was still working on the case, even though he'd retired. Shannon seems to have lied to his partner, Chris Peters, saying he was leaving for a few weeks for some R & R in Florida."

"Why would he do that?" Vincent asked.

"Good question," I said.

CHAPTER EIGHT

After two days of getting nowhere chasing down leads Chris Peters provided, a morning workout seemed in order.

The Solstice Fitness Center, on Broadway between East 19th and 20th, had little in common with my gym of choice, Bing's, where boxers and businessmen in sweats worked the bag and wore out machines. At Bing's you got a high-school phys ed feel and equipment often in worse shape than you were; you could rent a stained towel with holes for a buck, and endure lockers so small that you soon learned to arrive already in your sweats, unless you didn't mind going straight to the dry cleaners for a post-workout press of your incredibly wrinkled suit.

The Solstice, on the other hand, sported three levels with a top floor suspended over the main one where men and women pedalled stationery bikes and climbed ropes and ran in place like the starting gun of the New York Marathon would go off any second. Clients male and female in matching gray-and-white togs from the in-house boutique slow-jogged over to the juice bar or maybe for their massage. Disco on formidable speakers rivaled the sound level of the Tube's techno tripe, and the locker room was operating-room clean, the lockers themselves roomy, with towels included.

The endless array of equipment gleamed like a 1930s Hollywood-movie nightclub, with all the weight machines, treadmills and Stairmasters you could ever hope for, though no bags to punch. Personal trainers supervised about a third of the clientele, and in various areas coaches worked with groups.

It cost thirty bucks for a one-time workout, which made me regret not going on expense account. I was the sole soul in sweats from home, and easily the oldest person there. I put in a good workout and the six-foot guy about thirty who'd checked me in came over as I sat on the edge of a leg-weight machine, toweling off.

"What do you think, Mr. Hammer?" His voice was as husky as he was, muscular but not muscle-bound, a blandly handsome bullet-headed guy in a black t-shirt, matching polyester sweat pants and gray sneakers. He had a name tag that said ROD and a whistle around his neck. "Is Solstice for you?"

"I like all this equipment," I said. "Where I been going, the machines seem tied up half the time."

"We have a special going."

"Yeah?"

"Fifteen thousand a year. Regularly twenty-five."

Bing's was fifty bucks a month. Of course, I had to pay for towels.

I stood, wrapped the towel around my neck. "You wouldn't happen to know who I am, would you?"

"You're Mr. Hammer."

That's what I thought.

"My badge is in my locker," I said, which was a good way to make him think I was a cop without lying. He didn't have to know it was a private investigator's buzzer. "Casey Shannon was a member here, right?"

His expression didn't shift at all. "That was in the papers and on TV. He was killed, huh? Terrible."

Rod here didn't know *how* terrible. Pat Chambers was holding back the exact cause of death—"blow to the chest" was as far as the statement to the press went.

"Terrible," I agreed. "You mind answering a few questions, Rod?"

"No." He gestured toward where I'd checked in. "We can go in the office if you like…"

"This is fine right here. How long had Lt. Shannon been a member? Your rates are pricey on a civil servant's pay."

The trainer shrugged. "He had a trial membership, three months. It was almost up."

No, completely up. Now.

"Rod, how did he get along here?"

"He was like you, Mr. Hammer. Really good shape for his age."

Thanks a bunch, I thought.

I asked, "I mean, did he make any friends in particular?"

His smile was on the vacant side. "Oh yes. They didn't come in together or anything, but he always seemed to be here when Mr. Colby…Mr. Vincent Colby?…was in for a workout."

I was fishing and surprised to get so immediate a bite.

"I'm acquainted with Mr. Colby," I said. "Does he have a regular workout time?"

"He does. Three times a week, late afternoon Monday, Wednesday and a little earlier on Friday. Or he did. You may not be aware that Mr. Colby had an accident a few weeks ago, and hasn't been in since. But I'm sure, when he's recovered, he'll be back at it. He's a natural athlete. Played rugby at Princeton."

Harvard, actually.

"Tell me, Rod—would they ever work out together, Colby and Shannon?"

"Sometimes. They seemed friendly. Conversed. Not warm, but…people concentrate on their personal programs here. Of course, that brought them together in itself, since they had the same personal trainer."

"Who would that be?"

"Mashy."

"Pardon?"

"Mashy Sakai. Well, Masahiko Sakai—we just call him Mashy for short. Very proud to have him on staff."

"Oh?"

The trainer nodded. "He's achieved the final Dan level of Judan. That's—"

"Tenth-degree black belt."

"That's right. But Mashy does more than just teach martial arts with us. Oh, he includes that in the training, but as part of an overall fitness program, if you're interested. He's here right now, if you'd like to talk to him. Just finishing up a class on the second floor."

The black-trimmed white room upstairs that I slipped into was divided in half, one section with polished wood flooring, for exercises, the rest shielded by a green mat, for sparring. Each wall had a framed kanji print. Along the periphery of the matted area, a dozen students watched as a little slender round-faced man in his fifties, wearing the traditional loose-fitting uniform called a *karategi*, was squared off with a much larger, younger man similarly attired—of course, the larger, younger man was not wearing a black belt, which proved a factor.

The two faced each other poised for hand-to-hand combat. The small round-faced man made a quick sidestep, placing his right leg behind the bigger man's left leg, taking him down with a *wham*.

Both men rose, bowed, then the shorter one said, "Now that move, the *ōuchi gari*, or great inner reap, is an effective, simple way to bring your opponent down...unless he or she anticipates you and employs an *ashi barai*, a foot sweep. So try a hooking motion, not a reaping one."

They went through the routine again, with the *sensei* demonstrating that slight variation as the bigger man *whomped* down once more, poor bastard. Again they rose, bowed. The student returned to the periphery with the others.

Their teacher reminded them of the time and day of their next class, bowed, dismissed them, and they bowed in return, then trooped out, looking beaten and tired. Their *sensei* didn't appear to have broken a sweat.

The martial arts teacher turned to me—I was over on the slick wood floor, watching—as if he'd known I was there all along. Perhaps he had. His smile was almost angelic as he approached and held his hand out.

"Mr. Hammer," he said.

I took the hand, shook it, neither of us trying to impress the other, and he took it back.

"You're Mr. Sakai."

A head bow. "Call me Mashy. Everyone does, even my wife."

I looked at him curiously. "Did, uh, Rod give you a call that I was heading up to see you?"

Tiny shrug. "No, I just recognize you. From the papers and TV."

Well, he *was* over fifty.

"How can I be of service, Mr. Hammer?"

No need to talk badges with this guy.

"If you follow the papers," I said, "you probably know your client, Casey Shannon, was killed recently."

"Murdered. Yes." His expression turned somber. "A shame. Good man. Fine man. But I felt he was at Solstice under…false pretenses."

"Really? Why is that?"

His smile was a fleeting thing as he gestured toward the mat. "Shall we sit?"

We went over and sat like Indians, the Mick and the Jap. Half a lifetime ago we might have been in foxholes in the same war. Different foxholes.

Sakai picked right back up. "I believe he was here not seeking fitness, but to investigate another student of mine."

"Vincent Colby."

"Yes." He raised a gentle palm. "I should not have qualified that. When he first came to Solstice, Lt. Shannon came to me privately and asked a few questions."

"What, specifically?"

"Nothing specific. Generalities. What was my opinion of Vincent Colby as a person? I said I found him affable and hard-working, a good student. I explained that my context was not sufficient to discern more. I asked him what he was looking for. His answer was…remarkable."

"Oh?"

"He said he was looking for a killer."

I nodded, thinking about that. "Was there hostility between Colby and Shannon? Tension?"

"No. They were friendly. Not warm…" A faint smile. "…other than the sweat we work up here."

Said the guy who didn't seem to be able to work up a sweat.

"So I would say," the *sensei* said, "Lt. Shannon was not certain of Mr. Colby. Was Vincent Colby a good man or a bad man? Or, like so many of us, something in between? The lieutenant sought the answer."

"Is Colby a good student? Would you say he's proficient?"

Several emphatic nods. "Yes. One of my best. Took right to it."

I thought about that for a while and the *sensei* patiently waited for me.

Then I asked, "Is it difficult to kill someone with karate, Mr. Sakai?"

I thought the quick shift in subject might throw him; but this was not an easy man to throw in any sense of the word. His immediate response was only to say, "Call me Mashy, please, Mr. Hammer."

"Yeah, and I'm Mike. But is it?"

"Possible to kill with martial arts techniques? Certainly. Not so simple as on television and in the motion pictures, but…yes."

"Is there a karate move that could cave in a man's chest?"

He actually blinked. Once. "What a specific question, Mike."

"Is there?"

"I teach various aspects of martial arts here. If you are familiar with such things, you probably know I was sharing judo moves with my students when you came in. But I can assure you I have never taught that…*particular* move to any student, ever. Including Mr. Colby."

"What particular move?"

He sat silently for perhaps ten seconds, which is longer than it sounds. Try it. Then finally he spoke, quietly. Gravely.

"It is known as *migi-hiza age-ate ryo-ken ryo-soku hiki-oroshi*."

"That's a mouthful in any language."

He nodded, once. "A lot of words for a simple move, one that is useful in particular in close quarters. It is a concealed *bunkai*, a move hidden in plain sight—a self-defense technique that can save a life…and take one."

"What the hell is it exactly?"

His shrug was barely perceptible. "You pull your opponent's head down and simultaneously bring up a knee to his chest. Swiftly. Powerfully."

I frowned. "And that can kill?"

"With sufficient force applied, yes. The energy moves up from the feet to the knee, delivering a blow to the soft tissue under the rib cage while the opponent's head is held in a stationary position."

"Judas."

"The ribs are driven back through the lungs and solar plexus, shocking the nervous system. Enough force can be generated to equal two cars colliding head on at thirty-five miles an hour. If I may be somewhat pedantic…"

"Pedantic away."

"Just below the chest, the solar plexus is comprised of a dense bundle of nerve cells and supportive tissue. This is the abdominal cavity's autonomic nerve center, a concentrated bundle of nerve cells and supporting tissue—ganglia, interconnected neurons – that through their linkage with other nervous system bundles, allow disruption of visceral functioning for other organs, including the heart muscle."

"Causing death."

"Causing death, again—with proper force. If proper is the right word. This is nothing I would ever teach a student, or even mention, of course."

"Of course."

"But perhaps you would like me to show you a move to counter it?"

"Uh…yeah. *Oh* yeah."

As I came in through the office door, Velda was at her desk, on the phone, saying, "Here he is now, Pat."

I hung up my coat and hat, blew her a kiss, went on into my inner chamber, and took the call at my desk.

"We have another homicide," Pat's voice said.

"Well, isn't that what you're captain of?"

"A specific kind of homicide."

"…Shit. Not…"

"Another crushed chest cavity. A woman named Jasmine Jordan, a black call girl who worked out of an apartment house on East 78th. She had a whole damn floor to herself and her clients."

"Hell. At least she didn't work at Colby, Daltree & Levine."

His laugh was short and harsh. "Doesn't mean she didn't *know* somebody there. The Jordan woman was thirty and on Vice's radar, but this current operation was new to them. Other residents, none of whom were thrilled by Ms. Jordan's presence in the building, saw respectable-looking gents in business suits arrive by limo or cab, and later get picked up the same way."

"Do we know when she died? Who found her?"

"Anonymous tip. Female voice. Maybe a co-worker who found her and called it in, then got the hell out. Died last night between midnight and three a.m. is the initial read. Autopsy is today and we'll know more."

I grunted. "*Somebody's* ambitious. That's three kills in forty-eight hours…Vincent Colby could've been one of her well-heeled johns, you know."

I could almost hear his eyes narrowing. "Mike—I thought you were working for his father."

"I am. But young Colby's the linkage between all of the *other* kills, and anyway he's on my mind. I just got back from checking up on him at that high-class health club."

I told Pat that Shannon appeared to have been getting next to Colby as part of investigating those two suspicious homicides— the rape victim secretary who'd been strangled and the boiler-room broker who got run over in a parking garage.

"Shannon suspected him," Pat said.

"Would appear so. Those kills were a couple of stones in Casey's shoe, keeping him from walking carefree into retirement."

"He's carefree now," Pat said bitterly.

I shifted in my swivel chair. "Something you should know about Vincent Colby, buddy, if you don't already. He's a karate student. Apparently a fairly proficient one."

And I could hear his chair squeak as he sat forward. "Isn't *that* interesting. Could these crushed chests be the result of a karate move of some kind? I always figured that 'killing blow' stuff was just nonsense from the movies."

"Colby's trainer at the Solstice Fitness Center says it *is* possible. Not as easy as people think, but…yeah."

"Does the trainer know what he's talking about?"

"He's a tenth-degree black belt."

"Oh. Well, I guess I'll take his word for it."

"And, Pat, he says it's not anything he's ever taught a student. He says there are ways to kill with karate that are hiding in plain sight."

His laugh was rueful. "Sounds like you're already getting ahead of me on this one, Mike."

"I don't have a desk littered with other homicides to keep track of. But you were man enough to call me and let me know the Jasmine Jordan development. I'll keep you in the loop. Hell, you *are* the loop on this one."

"I appreciate that, Michael. Don't you go killing anybody who I'd rather see face the shame of a trial and a life behind bars."

"Do my best, Patrick."

"Oh, one other thing—Vincent Colby has an alibi for last night. Not much of one, but he has one."

"Which is what?"

"Daddy dearest says his beloved only child was tucked in a wee little bed. That makes two shitty alibis young Colby came up with—his girl friend for the Kraft kill, and now his old man, for a dead hooker whose classy clientele may well have included Vince."

"He prefers Vincent, Pat."

"Fuck him," Pat said, and hung up.

Vance Colby and I were once again seated opposite on respective two-seater sofas in the cavernous office that showed few signs of work ever being done, the fire again throwing orange and black reflections. Neither coffee nor brandy were offered this trip. I'd come unannounced, though my wealthy client hadn't hesitated to tell the Ice Lady to send me in.

"My son was at home all evening, Mike," he said, perhaps a bit too casually, arms folded as he leaned back on the plush over-stuffed sofa."

"Is it possible he slipped out while you were asleep?"

His shrug was brief. "I'll tell you what I told the police. I have trouble sleeping some nights, and last night was one of them. I was up till dawn watching television and reading, and would have known if he left. I wound up sleeping till noon, coming in late. Good thing I'm the boss."

"Good thing."

He gestured with an open hand. "If you'd like the name of the films I watched on American Movie Classics, I can provide them. And the book was *Bonfire of the Vanities*."

Somehow that made his alibi for his son seem only that much more negligible.

"No," I said, "I'll take your word for it."

That was a lie, but he was my client, and I'd banked his check.

"Several servants can back me up," he said, "if need be."

That was marginally better than the names of movies *TV Guide* could give him and a book he probably read months ago. But a guy with that kind of bread could spare however much it took to make a loyal servant even more loyal. That could mean good money in a murder case.

"Anyway, Mike—Vincent's medication at night puts him into a deep sleep. Almost a sedative."

I leaned forward. The flames were making abstract, flickering designs on his face, where his lingering thin-mustached smile seemed sickly to me.

I said, "Mr. Colby...Vance...if you no longer wish to engage me in this matter, I will understand. I will even return your retainer, minus a few expenses."

"Why would I do that?"

"Because there have been three murders since I undertook this job," I said, "including this call girl who died while you say your son was sleeping last night. And I'm old-fashioned—murders on my watch piss me off. Plus, they're bad for business."

"Your point eludes me, Mike."

"The point is that if you're lying to me about Vincent being home last night, all night...or if I discover that your son is responsible for these killings, *any* of these killings…I intend to turn him over to Captain Pat Chambers."

He was nodding. "Of the Homicide Division. Yes, I spoke with him earlier. Well, I would expect you to."

"Captain Chambers was a close friend of Lt. Shannon's. Pat will make sure that—if your son is guilty—Vincent will spend the rest of his life in prison."

"That doesn't worry me."

"Really."

"Yes, my son *is* innocent." His brow tensed. "And I very much *want* you on the case, Mike, clearing my boy."

I sighed. Patted my knees. Stood.

"So be it," I said.

He stood, too, and offered his hand and I shook it. A firm shake, but moist. The old man's smile looked like a sculptor slipped with his chisel and hadn't quite pulled it off.

I went out, winked at the Ice Lady, whose pursed-lipped, crinkled-chin reaction was at least technically a smile, and started to head out. Earlier, I'd again noticed that Vincent's office appeared empty.

But now the heir to the Colby throne was in, behind his desk, while a figure that I was pretty sure was William Owens, managing director of the firm, stood with his back to me, getting the Riot Act read to him. Vincent's angry voice, though muffled, was booming behind the glass, what he was saying unclear, but his rage unmistakable.

The little blonde Red Riding Hood in big-framed glasses was goggling from behind her receptionist desk, looking alarmed. I raised a hand to calm her and headed toward that office, but I hadn't made much progress before Owens, flushed and tearful, came bounding out.

Owens saw me and our eyes locked. Still moving, he said in a breathy rush, "I don't know *what* he was going on about! He just went *off!*"

Vincent came charging up behind Owens, and turned him around like a naughty child and shook him like such children once were shaken, in what I'm told were less enlightened times.

"Screw up like that again," Vincent was snarling, "and your ass is gone from here. Understand? *Gone!*"

Vincent, still holding onto this supposed friend by a shoulder, drew his other hand back in a fist, poised to punch. I got between them and the fist froze long enough for me to grab the wrist brandishing it.

"Go," I said to Owens, who scurried, muttering, "Thank you," heading out into the boiler room in a blur of striped shirt and orange suspenders.

Vincent's face was damn near scarlet, his eyes big and bulging, his nostrils flaring, like a rearing horse. The musky smell of his cologne—Obsession?—came off him like steam.

"You let go of me, Hammer! Let go of me or—"

I let go of him.

Then I slapped him.

The Ice Lady must have called her boss, because Colby was there in seconds, moving faster than a man his age really should.

"What are you *doing*, Mike?" my client demanded.

Vincent was standing there, dazed, weaving, rubbing his cheek, blinking like somebody who got soap in his eyes.

"What *you* should have," I said, "when he was a lot younger."

I glanced back like Lot's wife and saw the father walking his shaken son into the nearby glassed-in office. As I made my way through the boiler room, all eyes were on me, even the ones in headsets engaged in the latest cold calls.

I saw a lot of smiles.

CHAPTER NINE

Velda and I caught an early dinner at P.J. Moriarty's on Sixth and 52nd at Radio City before the mahogany-paneled steak-and-chophouse got really busy.

It wouldn't take long for that endless parade of bar stools to fill up, and for the conversation to build to a friendly din, punctuated by the occasional popped cork or dropped dish or clatter of silverware. Soon the red-leather banquettes—one of which we'd easily snagged—would become prime real estate.

I had the corned beef and cabbage while Velda got a small chef's salad with turkey, which is probably all you need to know about either of us. The only business we discussed had to do with an arson investigation for one of our best insurance clients. We didn't go over the Colby job until the coffee had arrived and I was done with the cheesecake. Velda had two petite bites – the kind of cheesecake she embodied taking discipline.

I filled her in on the trip to the Solstice Fitness Center and my return visit to Colby, Daltree & Levine.

"Either Vincent is playing me," I said, "or somebody is trying to frame him. We've got death by a forbidden martial arts move and young Colby studying with a tenth-degree black belt trainer. We've got a series of murders all connected in some way to our client's son, with one of the victims a cop who was looking at Colby like Ahab eyeing that white whale."

At the end of her workday, Velda still looked fresh, the arcs of her dark hair touching the wide shoulders of a lime silk blouse that needed no pads to be in fashion.

She frowned in thought over the rim of her coffee cup from which she'd just sipped. "Do you think Casey Shannon was convinced of Colby's guilt?"

I shook my head. "Probably not. Casey was still investigating."

"What kind of unofficial case file did your friend Shannon leave behind?"

"Nothing's been found, and Pat and his crew—including the top forensics guys—gave Casey's pad a thorough shake."

"And?"

"And came up with bupkis...at least as far as I know. Pat is stingier with information than usual."

"Any chance they missed it?"

I shrugged. "Always a chance of that. And if Casey *had* come up with something—either indicating Colby's guilt, or someone else's..."

She was nodding. "And hadn't *moved* on it."

"...it could still be somewhere in that apartment."

She sipped coffee, her expression growing thoughtful. Then she said: "The police are finished with the place, aren't they? Can't you get in and have a look around yourself, Mike?"

I smirked. "It's still a crime scene, baby. Closed off with good ol' yellow tape with DO NOT CROSS in big black letters."

"Why, don't you have scissors?"

That deserved a smile and I gave her one. "Normally, Pat would let me in. But he's only dealing me cards he thinks he can use my help on. He wants Casey's killer himself. He doesn't want me spoiling his fun."

Half a smirk dug briefly into a pretty cheek. "Because you'd just kill the bastard, whereas Pat wants to prolong the agony."

"Some people just aren't nice."

A waitress came by and refilled my coffee. I nodded thanks, then stirred in sugar and cream and said, "There won't be any cop on the door or anything…but I could be seen by a neighbor, working my little lock-pick routine. Still, it might be worth the risk."

She gestured with a tapered hand, its nails bright red. "Why not get some help? Call Shannon's peach-fuzz partner, Chris Peters. You said he was pretty broken up about his mentor buying it. If they were *that* close, good chance he has a key."

I sipped and smiled. "Doll, you could get by on looks alone… but you don't. That is a damn good suggestion."

"Thank you. Want my company?"

I shook my head. "If I can get hold of Chris…and he gave me his card, with his home number on the back, offering to help if I needed any on this thing…two will be company, and three a crowd."

"Thank you very much."

"Hey, honey, trust me—I have other things you can do for me."

Both eyebrows went up. "I bet you do."

I let that pass. "We are assuming this Roger Kraft character was the driver of the Ferrari."

"A sound assumption, I think."

"I agree. But *why* was he killed?"

Her eyes narrowed. "Maybe somebody hired the job and was tying off a loose end."

I narrowed mine back at her. "Maybe. But what if Kraft had a grudge against young Colby himself? Clearly that was no accident outside Pete's Chophouse, not when Roger Dodger was out driving a sports car that didn't belong to him, while wearing a fake beard and pony tail."

She had a slow nod going. "Did that second-in-command guy at the brokerage, Owens, hire Kraft maybe? Owens and Colby were arguing about something, you said, and it got heated."

"True," I admitted.

"Also, Kraft was working on Owens's car, which happens to be the red Ferrari that almost got a lot redder. Could that be the reason for the office dust-up—Colby learned Owens tried to have him killed...?"

She shook her head and her hair went wild, then tamed itself.

"No," she said firmly, answering her own question. "That's dumb. Colby would've called the cops on his 'friend.'"

"Probably."

She cocked her head. "Just probably?"

I gestured with an open hand. "As irrational as Don't-Call-Me-Vince has been lately, who knows? But more likely it's some work thing and just demonstrates what a loose cannon that concussion's made out of our client's baby boy."

Her nod was in slow motion. "I can buy that."

"But, again, doll—*why* was Kraft killed, and who *did* it...? If Pat has any ideas about that, he's sure not sharing them."

The waitress stopped by again and Velda held up a hand, preferring not to have her coffee cup refilled. We'd both had enough caffeine already to fuel the evening ahead.

Velda said, "All we know about Kraft is that he was part of a heist crew, and after this new heat, with their driver turning up dead? The accomplices will be in the wind."

"Most likely. And if Kraft hadn't been killed the same chest-crushing way as Shannon and that call girl? I would think tracking that end of things might pay off."

"But we're obviously dealing with one killer."

"Right again. This doesn't seem to have anything to do with smash-and-grab bank jobs."

Her eyebrows rose contemplatively. "I have my own police contacts. You want me to dig into the late Mr. Kraft and his life and times?"

"Damn straight. You still know some of the undercover girls in Vice, right?"

Her dark hair bounced as she nodded. "Yeah. Nobody's around from when I worked there, a million years ago, but yes, I have contacts. And I know some of the working girls, from that undercover job a couple of years back. Let me guess—that dead upscale hooker, what was her name?"

"Jasmine Jordan. But you're ahead of me on this."

"I am. I'll see what I can find out about her and maybe we can get a line on her patrons. If one of them is Vincent Colby, we could be getting close to an answer his father—our client—won't like."

My grin was nasty. "I warned him this afternoon—told him I intend to follow this wherever it leads. The old man had his chance to bail."

She raised a forefinger. "Something else."

"Shoot. You should pardon the expression."

"We're assuming *one* killer because of the distinctive method of murder."

"Yes we are."

"But we're leaving out the first two kills—the raped, strangled secretary from the Colby firm, and the suspicious-as-hell hit-and-run in that parking ramp of all places, taking down a broker from Colby, Who's It and What's It. Let's call *them* murders, too."

"Let's."

She leaned forward, keeping her voice down. The restaurant was starting to fill up and murder talk required a little discretion.

"Obviously," she said, "the first two homicides are related to Colby and his business. But they lack the signature kills of the other victims. Those could be the work of someone else. They don't even have to be the acts of a single perpetrator. It's even possible we are looking for *three* murderers."

I winced. "You're giving me heartburn, baby."

"It's the corned beef and cabbage." She shook her head again and the dark locks shimmered. "This is going to bleed into tomorrow, Mike."

"I know it will."

The check came.

I said, "Call the temp agency and get somebody in to fill in for you. Maybe that little Asian cutie is available."

She arched a single eyebrow this time. "Fill in for me *how?*"

I smiled and raised both palms in surrender. "Honey, nobody could ever really fill in for you, not even on a temporary basis."

"Right answer."

Chris Peters was on board almost immediately. He and his wife and baby girl lived in Brooklyn, so I had to wait for him a while, but it would be worth it. Turned out he did have a key to his late partner's pad, and—like me—he didn't want to leave this thing to Pat.

"Mike, don't quote me," he said, when I picked him up in my souped-up black Ford heap near the subway station in Tudor City on East 42nd. "But I'm not in sync with Captain Chambers on this one."

"How so, Chris?"

"Let's just say I'm less anxious to bring Casey's killer in alive."

The slender blond cop was dressed for work—a tailored suit jacket with room around the waist to hide bulges of gun and gear. The unofficial NYPD policy was, "Dressed for a meeting, ready for mayhem." I was garbed similarly, though my ensemble was set off by my porkpie fedora; Batman doesn't go out without his cowl, does he? A kid like Chris, even on detective duty, went bareheaded.

I parked on a cross street a couple of blocks from Shannon's apartment building. Our breaths were smoking. As we walked quickly along, nudged by the chill, I mulled what the young cop had said.

We'd just paused before heading behind the place, where Chris knew of a rear door adjacent to the service elevator. Luckily the building was on a corner and the doorman wouldn't get wise to us.

I said, "You leave the vigilante shit to me, kid. You got a career going on the PD. Me, I got asked to leave a long time ago."

"You were a cop once, Mike?"

"Most PIs were. I was making too much noise on the street when I was your age, and they stuck me on a desk. Which was the same as firing me, far as I was concerned."

"I hear you."

I put a hand on his shoulder. "If we're approached in there, you show your badge and make the trouble go away. I have a badge too, if it comes to that, but it says 'Private Investigator' on it."

He was nodding, breath pluming. "But either way, if we're caught at this, I play the cop card."

"Damn skippy. You have a key given to you by your late partner. You have a right to cross a police crime scene barricade. You'll get your ass chewed if it gets back to Captain Chambers, but he won't pursue it."

"Okay."

"And if he does, I'll convince him I talked you into this."

In well under five minutes, we were on Shannon's floor. The expected crime scene tape was there, in a dramatic X, which we ducked under, after Chris unlocked the door.

The forensics team had left the place in good shape. Beyond the taped outline of where Shannon had fallen near and against the couch, no sign of their work remained. Even the dust of the black-graphite fingerprint powder had been cleaned away, which isn't easy.

"God," Chris said, looking pale. "It's like nothing ever happened. It's like Casey might just walk in on us."

The bizarre outline on the floor and up onto the front of the couch said otherwise. Because Shannon had been slumped with his head forward, the outline had a ghastly decapitated look.

"Chris," I said, "I don't want to toss the place. Pros have gone over it. We won't be gutting cushions or dumping out bureau drawers onto the floor."

"No need," his partner said. "I know Casey's ways. He kept private files on open cases, even when the rest of us had moved on. Photocopied stuff he shouldn't have. Made his own notes. Took his own pictures."

I nodded. "And Pat and the forensics bunch weren't necessarily looking for any such file. They were processing a murder scene. But if our assumptions are right, the file on that pair of unsolved homicides, and any notes on Vincent Colby, could be here."

Chris held his hands out, palms up. "Worth a look. Worth a *damn* good look."

The corner with the roll-top desk seemed a good place to start.

"I'll go over this thing," I said, opening it up, "and see if I can find any hidden compartments. These old behemoths have more secrets than a haunted house."

The remark lingered oddly. We were, in a way, in a haunted house right now.

The nearby file cabinet was a dark-stained oak vertical four-drawer affair. Supervising above were three framed items—two commendations for valor on either side of the color framed 8" by 10" of President Reagan, signed to Casey.

"Take a look at those," I said.

Chris took them down; all three were sealed in with brown paper, nothing taped to the backs. I told him to hang 'em back up, and he did.

"You go through the file cabinet," I said. "I'm sure they checked everything, but maybe Casey had a system where he filed things under names that didn't match their contents."

He checked each drawer. Every one was empty.

I said, "Damn. Pat must have confiscated them."

"I'll out take the drawers and see if anything's taped in back, in the cabinet itself."

That seemed a little desperate to me. Casey would have wanted easy access to that particular file and that made for a lot of trouble getting to it. Maybe it lay under the bottom file drawer, though. All you'd have to do is pull the drawer out and underneath would be the secreted file.

But no.

Nothing.

I fared little better. I did find a secret compartment but only family photos were within, Casey's late wife, his kids when they were…kids. I collected these and dropped them in my suit coat pocket. The grown versions of those youngsters would be coming in for the services, in a few days. Shannon would get the complete police funeral with honor guard and a sea of blue in attendance.

There'd be an End of Watch call, officers from Casey's division gathering around a car's police radio as a dispatcher issued a call to Lt. Shannon with silence the response. A second call would go out and get the same silent response. Then an officer who'd worked with him—probably Chris or maybe

Ben Higgins—would respond that Lt. Shannon could not answer because the officer had fallen in the line of duty.

I swallowed and abandoned the roll-top search. Chris had finished the file cabinet as well, with equally unsuccessful results. We started in on the bookcase and went through every page of every book. We occasionally found a random piece of paper—a receipt from Coliseum Books, a bookmark, a slip of paper with a grocery list or some work reminder on it.

Nothing worth finding, really, just the routine detritus of a life lived.

I sat on the couch with Casey's body outline next to me. Chris stood in front of me, eyes avoiding the ghost of his partner.

"Fool's errand?" he asked.

"Too early to know." I sighed. "We're going over ground the forensics guys, and for that matter Pat Chambers, have already gone over good. We have only one advantage."

"What?"

"You."

The young cop gestured to himself, frowning, then said again, "What?"

"You worked with the man. You worked with him on *this case*. Casey knew he was poking around in the dirty secrets of a powerful Wall Street firm. Politics stink sometimes, but they're real and they have an impact on cops. The Commissioner says, 'Drop it.' When you don't, the Chief of Police says, 'We've got a nice beat for you to walk in Staten Island. You'll love it.'"

His arms were folded but a hand was up rubbing his chin. "You mean, if anybody anywhere knows what Casey Shannon was thinking, in the weeks before…before this *happened*…it's…"

"It's you, kid." I stood. Gestured toward the rest of the apartment. "Let's look at the places the pros wouldn't think of."

He frowned. "There can't be many of those."

"Well, hell, let's try anything that strikes you as a possibility. Then we'll look everywhere else, *harder* than the pros did. You're the one whose partner got killed, not them."

We went through the cupboards. On our hands and knees, we sorted through the area under the sink where cleaning products were kept. Checked to see if there was a plastic bottle that was empty but had something rolled up in it. When that was a no go, we tried the refrigerator, where the dead man's food was waiting never to be eaten. I figured maybe the box of frozen pizza, still in its plastic wrapper, might give up a prize, and it did.

A frozen pizza.

Back into the freezer it went, while we headed into the bedroom. We gave it a thorough going over, even though I knew everything we were doing had been done before by an experienced team and a certain captain of Homicide. We looked under the mattress and the bed itself, like maybe a cuckolded husband was hiding under there. Went through the nightstand, pulling out the drawer, checking every damn thing and place you could imagine.

A linen closet had us going through towels and sheets like Lawrence of Arabia after a new look. The bathroom had the usual supplies and bath towels and clothes; the medicine cabinet contained everything from a few prescription meds to razor blades and corn pads. A clothes closet gave us nothing special, just more of the specially-cut-for-a-cop suits and some sports clothes, including an ill-advised Hawaiian shirt. A cubbyhole above the closets had suitcases, which we dragged down and went through and found lots of empty.

All these closets reminded me I hadn't bothered with the front one. We wandered back into the living room, feeling defeated, and I looked in at fall and winter coats and a shelf with a collection of hats that put Casey on the same dinosaur list as Pat and me, only Casey was already extinct.

In the bottom of the closet were galoshes and sandals, but also something else.

I knelt. Two good-size unopened boxes—one low-slung, longer than it was wide, much like the one Velda's VCR had come in; the other was a cardboard cube with something heavy inside. Both were from Radio Shack.

"Tandy 1000 TX," I read from the lower-riding box. "Computer?"

"Yeah." Chris was kneeling too. "And that's a monitor to go with it. I think the keyboard's in the box with the computer."

"The packaging looks new. Did Shannon know how to use one of these gizmos? Velda has a word processor at the office."

Chris nodded. "Yeah, he had one at work, too." His brow furrowed. "You know, if Casey's file was on a floppy disk, all that material would be in Pat's hands by now. I think we're on that fool's errand we talked about."

I glared at the boxes. "Let's get in these things."

We hauled the boxes out, popped them open, but it soon seemed obvious this was their first trip out in the wilds. They were covered in taped plastic, which we removed. We wrestled with the things, but they were new, all right. Even smelled new.

And there were no floppy disks at all.

"Okay, kid," I said, as I slid the boxes back in the closet. I stood and closed the door on our great discovery. "We better get out of here before somebody calls the cops."

"Mike…do you think anybody would mind, if…" He seemed embarrassed, suddenly. "No, I shouldn't. But…"

"Shouldn't what?"

He walked over, tentatively, and pointed to the framed photo of Reagan on the wall above the file cabinet.

"Casey said, after he was gone…he wanted me to have that picture. Said his boys are a couple of know-it-all liberals and…" He swallowed thickly. "You think it's okay if I take it now?"

I was over there quick. "Take it down."

"Thanks, Mike."

"Save your thanks. Get that thing down for me."

He reached up and plucked the framed picture off the wall and, puzzled, handed it to me.

I turned it over. Looked at how the back was sealed up with brown paper. It didn't look tampered with, and the seal was tight. I was probably on another fool's errand. But I tore the paper off anyway, getting another confused frown out of Chris. A piece of gray car,dboard backing was inside. I pried that out with a thumb nail.

There, behind our president, was a 3½-inch unlabeled floppy disk.

I grinned. "Thank you, modern technology. Here, kid…you take Dutch's picture, I'll take the file we been looking for."

That was when the lights went out.

Blackness swallowed everything and neither of us said a word, barely able to get a gasp out. I heard the door open, but no light was on in the hall, either. I sensed somebody coming at me, and swung at where I thought that was, connecting with nothing.

Night vision started working itself in, thanks to the window by the roll-top onto a New York out there that was not suffering a blackout. The intruder was my size but not as heavy, almost certainly male, and Chris went for him but got straight-armed to the floor, a blow so hard and swift I felt the wind of it pass me.

Then hands were on the sides of my head, forcing it down, and I knew in a split second what was coming next, and remembered what *sensei* Sakai had taught me. I dropped the disk and grabbed the forearms of the attacker and I threw myself backward, taking the bastard along with me before that knee could rise up like a cannonball and make a caved-in corpse out of me. On the floor, on my back, I rocked back and put my foot on the fucker's chest and flung him over my head.

He landed hard, furniture jumping as if startled, but the attacker was quick, and he was up before me, but then Chris was coming at him again. A karate kick made more wind, a sweeping move that sent Chris flailing into the darkness. I came up behind the attacker, but he swung around and another straight-leg kick knocked me against the wall or maybe the closet door, I couldn't be sure.

Then the figure was gone, the slam of the door announcing his absence. I almost ran after him, but first checked Chris, who muttered, "I'm okay, I'm okay," though I could tell he was hurting.

I went to the door, opened it and—.45 in hand – stepped into a hall where no windows onto the street were there to aid night vision. Footsteps were receding, heading toward the elevator, around the corner, I thought.

I did not take pursuit. Not in the dark. Not with Chris in pain. And anyway, the only way I had to light up the world for a moment was a blind shot from the .45.

I was kneeling over the kid, gun still in hand, when the lights snapped on, mechanical sounds kicking in and starting back up, whirring noises that were climbing up to speed. I'd left the door to the hall open, and lights had come on out there, too. Had somebody hit the switch on the entire damn building—first off, then back on?

We were both breathing hard. I sat on the floor and Chris was doing the same.

That was when we noticed the floppy disk was gone.

"Shit," I said. "He must have been listening in the hall! Somehow he cued an accomplice to kill the lights. But how?"

"Radio Shack also sells walkie-talkies," Chris said glumly.

"Well, kid—at least he didn't take your Reagan picture."

We started to laugh. It beat crying.

CHAPTER TEN

The night mist was going to turn into something—the sky's rumbling stomach said so. Whether it would be rain or snow remained to be seen. Right now it just filled the air, giving soft halos to streetlights and a neon-reflecting slickness to the street, where headlights sent smudgy beams into a darkness that would only get darker.

That dust-up in the dark at Shannon's pad may have almost killed me, but that had been a matter of avoiding a knee to the chest; otherwise I felt fine and didn't figure I showed enough damage to attract Velda's attention when I headed for our regular back booth at the Olde English Tavern on Third Avenue. We'd agreed to meet at ten and I was on time. She was already there.

I slid in opposite her and noticed she was frowning, just a little. She was still wearing the lime silk blouse and forest-green skirt she'd worn to work, and looked just as fresh as when she'd walked in the door this morning.

"What happened to you?" she asked.

Apparently I didn't look so fresh.

I said, "I didn't think it showed."

Her eyes tightened. "You got a little limp going there."

"Come on, baby. I'm never limp around you."

All that got was a smirk.

She said, "Spill."

I spilled. Midway through the story, a waitress who knew me well enough to deliver a Canadian Club and ginger without asking did so. Velda showed nothing in her expression, not even concern. Well, she did wince when I reported that thrusting knee that tried to be my valentine.

She had a Manhattan going, which she sipped as I reported, and when I'd wrapped up, she said, "You can't be sure Casey's file was on that disk."

"Reasonable assumption," I said with a shrug. "It was a backup, probably, squirreled away for Chris to find when that framed photo came his way. Casey went to some trouble, sealing it up. Looked like it came straight from the framer's."

"You didn't see the guy who jumped you."

I shook my head, sipped the CC & ginger. "No. Just enough light from the window to make out the shape. Good size guy. My size. He took Chris down with some martial arts moves, which is no surprise, since this is clearly our Knees Up Mother Brown murderer."

The gag seemed appropriate in a pub.

Her eyes remained tight. "You didn't get any sense of the attacker, beyond being a male, and your size?"

"I got a whiff of his aftershave, his cologne, whatever. 'Obsession.'"

Her eyes opened a little. "Unless you were just smelling yourself."

Velda had got me a little bottle of the stuff for my birthday—

she thought the name was funny, considering my personality, plus she'd read in the *Times* that forest rangers in central India used the fragrance to lure a man-killing tiger out of the jungle, thanks to a certain pheromone used as an ingredient.

"I didn't know," she said, amused but her expression thoughtful, "that you'd started using it yet."

"I haven't," I said. "Not after you told me the secret ingredient was scraped from glands near a civet's anus."

She chuckled, but got serious again. "And your attacker tonight was wearing the stuff?"

"Yeah, unless he'd been giving a civet a rim job."

She almost did a spit take with the Manhattan.

But she managed to ask, "I don't suppose you know anybody who uses that cologne."

"Actually, doll, I do know of one."

"Well?"

"Our client's son."

"Vincent Colby?"

"Vincent Colby."

"Who," she said, "is about your size and is proficient, his *sensei* says, in martial arts. For a beginner, anyway."

"Roger that. Speaking of which, find out anything about the late, unlamented Roger Kraft?"

She nodded. "He had another profession, besides getaway car driver. He was a stuntman, working a lot of the films and TV shows shot in the city."

"He had the build for it," I said.

Velda glanced past me toward the front of the place, then patted the air with a palm. "Lily is just coming in the door. Be nice."

"Who's Lily? And I'm always nice."

Velda gave me a look. "Lily is the other call girl who worked out of that suite with Jasmine Jordan. She agreed to meet with you. Here's a picture of Jasmine Jordan, by the way. It tells a story."

Velda slid a color 5" by 7" studio photo across to me. It told a story, all right—a full-figure shot of a handsome, voluptuous woman with a milk chocolate complexion that seemed light against a dark chocolate leather catsuit and very high-heeled black shoes. In her right hand was a riding crop.

I tucked it away.

Velda had gone to intercept the young woman, and they stopped at the bar to get the newcomer a drink. She was tall and appeared to be slender, but was wrapped up in a tan hooded raincoat with only a little showing of what seemed to be a lot of long, permed platinum hair. Only nylons and glittery red shoes showed, like she'd just arrived back from the Land of Oz. She had entered from a dark night that was getting wet enough to justify the raincoat, but her big-lensed, white-framed sunglasses were less explainable, unless she was a movie star. If so, I didn't recognize her.

And if anonymity was what she was seeking—Lily, Velda had said her name was—it wasn't working. Everybody in the bar, which was half-full (as optimists like me would say) was looking at her. New Yorkers who won't give you a glance on the street were happy to stare indoors.

But then Lily and Velda tucked themselves in across from me in the booth and the pretty if somewhat hard young hooker was forgotten.

"This is my boss," Velda said, "Mike Hammer. You may have heard of him."

"Sorry, no," she said, in a little girl voice—the kind of Judy Holliday pipes that probably got some of her clients off. She tugged back the hood and revealed my prediction about a mass of curly permed white-blonde hair had been correct.

"Call me Mike," I said.

"Call me Lily," she said, with the tiniest smile.

"Thanks for talking to us, Lily. You were Jasmine's roommate?"

"We lived together," she said, with a nod. "I knew Ronnie since high school. That was her real name—or anyway Veronica was. Like the Ronettes? She was a couple years older than me. We both had bad family scenes and caught a bus together and got the hell out. We were a couple of runaways who got lucky."

"How so?"

Do I have to say that two girls who fell into a life of prostitution hardly qualified as "lucky"?

She frowned above the big sunglasses and asked, "You don't need the whole story, do you?"

"Just enough to get my feet under me, honey."

"Okay."

She sipped her drink, a Bloody Mary, and folded her hands; her nails were painted red, like Velda's, their sole similarity beyond being lookers.

"Well," she began, "a pimp approached us at the bus station and he took to both of us, right away. Thought we had potential. He trained us. For Ronnie, the S & M scene made a sweet set-up—she didn't even have to do the guys. Just punish them till they came. She worked out of various apartments over the past six or seven years."

"How old are you, Lily?"

"Twenty-seven."

She was good-looking, but you'd say thirty-seven.

"Ronnie had it better than me, because she worked at home," she continued. "Working at home is really great. I went to the clients, hotels mostly. My specialty was costumes. I dressed up like little girls. You know, schoolgirls. Catholic girls are really popular."

"I bet they are."

"I have a Little Bo Peep costume one regular really likes. Most of these clients just pleasure themselves. I hardly ever do the deed. And if I do, it costs them."

"Jasmine...Ronnie...never 'did the deed'?"

"No. She hated men. That's what was so cool about her being in that profession. No sex, and she mostly was the dominatrix."

Velda asked, "Never the submissive?"

"Much less often. But even then, it was bondage, discipline, not sex. Sometimes it got out of hand, though. She had one client... well, *everybody* has a client like that."

"Like what?" I asked.

"Who pays extra for you to go...too far."

"Tell me about this client."

She shrugged. "I don't know much. Don't know his name. But I do know he was rough. A real sadist. But the money was good, and he never went...*too* too far."

"And this bus-station pimp still gets his cut?"

She flashed a smile; her teeth were nice, on the small side. "No, that's part of what made us so lucky. He got killed. Some other pimp slit his throat."

He got his cut, after all.

She was saying, "Which is sad in a way, because he was good to us, way better than most. We've been freelance ever since. Solo venders, no organized ring, no pimp. We have arrangements with taxicab drivers, hotels, law firms, businesses, the M and B game."

Manufacturers and buyers.

"Our clients wear Brooks Brothers," she said. "I never walked a street in my life, Mike. Neither did Jasmine."

Maybe she *was* lucky. But Jasmine hadn't been.

I asked, "Did one of those Brooks Brothers types kill Jasmine, d'you think, Lily?"

Her forehead furrowed. "Almost has to have. She wouldn't let a stranger in. A cop with ID, maybe. It would be clients, mostly regulars. Sometimes referrals from those places I mentioned."

"Businesses. Was one of them Colby, Daltree & Levine?"

"No. Is that a law firm?"

"Brokerage. Was Vincent Colby a regular?"

She shrugged. "I don't know who that is. I stayed out of Ronnie's business. She stayed out of mine. She was discreet. But I'll tell you one suspicious thing."

"Please."

"She *did* keep a book, strictly for herself. A notebook, meticulous—neat rows of names, places, figures."

"For blackmail purposes?"

"No! She wasn't that kind of girl. It was to protect herself. She called it a life insurance policy."

Hadn't really paid off, had it?

"You need to understand the setup, Mike. We had the whole floor. We lived in one half, Jasmine did business in the other. I never brought anybody home."

"This notebook…"

"Gone. Somebody took it. Might be the cops, but I'd guess whoever did this terrible thing to her is who has it now." She sat forward, the big dark lenses staring at me. "Mike—Velda says you're a detective. That you're looking for whoever did this."

"I am. Jasmine isn't the killer's only victim—we know of two others, who died the same way. And it's possible another two were disposed of otherwise."

Her mouth tightened. "Disposed of."

"Sorry. That was a cold way to put it. You girls had been friends for a long time."

"We weren't friends, Mike."

"You weren't?"

She took the glasses off. The flesh around her eyes was swollen, puffy, and red; redder still were what had been the whites of her eyes. Lily had been crying. Lily had been crying her heart out.

"I loved Ronnie," she said. "And she loved me."

She began to sob and Velda put an arm around her, and gave me a tortured look. Lily had no tears left, but the crying? That may have only just started.

Finally it eased up, and she gave us her phone number, saying she'd do anything to help that she could. If we wanted a look at Jasmine's "dungeon," and their living quarters, she'd accommodate us, if we liked. I said we might take her up on that.

She asked, "Can you find the one who did this?"

"Count on it."

"I don't mean to insult you, Mike, but…you look like a man who could kill somebody if you felt like it."

Velda seemed amused by the hooker's good judge of character.

I said, "Are you sure you've never heard of me?"

Her little smile seemed almost embarrassed. "I remembered while we were talking. You killed that Penta character. It was on the news."

"I did."

The ravaged eyes bore in on me. "Will you kill Ronnie's killer, Mike?"

"I promised a friend I wouldn't."

"That's too bad. That's a shame."

"But this friend is a cop who will see that the killer goes away for a long, long time."

"That's something, anyway."

She put on the sunglasses and slipped out of the booth. Velda scooted out too, to give her a hug.

When Velda returned, she said, "That special client of Ronnie's…who liked to get rough. What's that tell you?"

"Well, two things come to mind. Vincent Colby frequents the Dungeon Room at the Tube."

"That's one."

"And those black eyes that Sheila Ryan habitually gets? We may have been reading that wrong. What if it's our client's son who's been battering that babe?"

"Our client's son who wears Obsession?" She half-smiled,

shook her head. "The one who knows some martial arts? Maybe after the hit-and-run outside Pete's Chophouse, the dark side of Vincent Colby came out to play."

I was nodding. "The *bunkai* knee-kick kills didn't start in till he'd had the concussion."

I got out of the booth, threw some bills down to cover the damage. Said, "You go home, doll. This long night isn't over yet."

Her hand found mine. "You must be dead on your feet, lover. Come home with me. Let's get some rest and start back in on this tomorrow."

I shook my head. "Our killer isn't taking any time off. I don't like the way the players in our little cast keep thinning. It's only eleven. Like the song says, I'll knock on your door around midnight."

"Around midnight," she said, not arguing.

The mist kept promising rain while the sky's occasional rumble made a threat out of it. Only the glowing signs of chain retailers (B. Dalton) and fast-food (Nathan's) burned through the haze to break the spell of the old Bohemian Village that lingered on tree-lined streets where the buildings were too low-slung to create a skyline. The wet night would not dissuade the dealers and muggers from frequenting Washington Square Park, though the former had the decency to set up shop on benches, while the latter clung to the darkness, the cops a no-show in an area mostly left to its own devices.

Yet the Village remained a state of mind, where rebels and outsiders, artists and scribblers, hustlers and dreamers, converged on disorganized streets that turned the grid of Manhattan into a game of pick-up sticks. You could still play chess here, catch a foreign film, groove to jazz, eat midnight pizza, and get hopelessly lost.

I was neither tourist nor newcomer to a part of town that said, "Go screw yourself," and, "Welcome," all at once. And knowing the growls and looks and downright refusals from cabbies who hated Village fares because of those goddamn streets down there, I drove myself—my black Ford always spooked residents into thinking it was an unmarked car, which only amused me.

The apartment I was looking for was on Morton Street, in a brick mid-block five-story with a fire escape riding its face. The trees along here were skimpy with autumn making way for winter, and parking on the street was scarce, but I found a spot two blocks down from my destination.

When I'd used the phone at the pub, I got the Ryan girl's friend, who she was staying with, who said Sheila was out but expected back shortly. The friend said I could come around, her voice chirpy and sociable and vaguely familiar. It still seemed that way, when she buzzed me up.

On the third floor, at number 302, I saw why: the blonde in her early twenties who answered the door – with her hair all permed and teased, as if Marilyn Monroe's hair had exploded but in a good way—was the Red Riding Hood receptionist/secretary from Colby, Daltree & Levine.

She wasn't wearing the big-lensed glasses tonight, but the eyes themselves were plenty big, their deep blue emphasized by a lot of darker blue eye shadow. She wore a form-fitting black dress with a pattern that it took me a while to discern was little gray screwdrivers, pointing up and pointing down alternately.

"Mr. Hammer," she said, the words emerging from a mouth so dark-red lipsticked it was damn near black, "you're lucky you caught me! I just got back from a date and I'd have been in bed."

That seemed a little ambiguous, but I didn't ask for an explanation. Was she on something? Maybe a little tipsy?

Hat in hand, I asked, "Is Ms. Ryan back?"

"No, but it shouldn't be too long. Come in, come in!"

I did, entering into a small living room with funky second-hand 1950s atomic furniture and a kitchenette where the dishes of a working week awaited attention. The wood floor had a central throw rug—black with colorful geometric shapes—and riding the pastel walls were a framed Andy Warhol print of Debbie Harry and original abstract paintings probably bought on a nearby street.

She deposited me on a comfy overstuffed Naugahyde two-seater sofa, then gestured to the kitchenette. "Can I get you a wine cooler or a light beer or anything?"

"No, I'm fine. Sorry to impose."

Her voice had a musical lilt. "Sheila should be along soon. Do you mind if I get out of these things?"

Was that a trick question?

"Not at all," I said.

A nearby amoeba-shaped coffee table, with boomerang designs, was scattered with *Cosmo*, *Vogue* and the *New Yorker*, from under which *Playgirl* cover boy Geraldo Rivera peeked. He was smiling at me, as if suppressing a wink. The second-hand store *Leave It to Beaver*-era furnishings struck me as a cheap way to put together a hip decor.

She came back with the make-up washed off, wrapped up in a belted white silk dressing gown that stopped at the knee. Without the war paint, she looked about sixteen. She plopped down next to me, sitting with her legs tucked under her and her arm along the sofa's upper edge.

"I know who you are," she said.

"Yeah, I'm the guy who came around Colby's a couple of times lately."

"No. I mean I know *who* you are."

I shrugged. "That makes two of us."

She frowned a little. "You mean you know who *I* am?"

Who's on first?

"Not really," I said. "But I know who *I* am. I'm Mike."

"I'm Julie Olsen."

"Pleased to meet you, Julie."

With the vaudeville routine out of the way, she moved on. "Sheila told me some things about you. Said you're famous, in a way."

"In a way."

Her chin came up and so did the corners of her mouth. "I told my daddy I'd met you—he called from Queens, where he and my mother are. He was impressed."

"He must impress easily."

She shook her head and all that blonde hair came along for the ride. "Not really. Sheila went back for a few more of her things."

I didn't follow that and my expression must have said so.

She explained: "Back to Gino's apartment, for more clothes and personal effects and stuff. Now that she's moved back in here. We were roomies before she moved in with Gino."

"Ah."

She frowned. Maybe for the first time, judging by that smooth face. "Did you know he used to abuse her? I mean, *really* abuse her, slap her around, smack her and stuff, with his fist sometimes."

"She's going with Vincent Colby now."

"She is. *He's* nice."

"He doesn't abuse her?"

"Oh no."

"I heard he likes it rough."

She blinked at me. "Likes what rough?"

"Sex. Or sex play, anyway."

Shrug. "I wouldn't know. He's *her* boyfriend."

I shifted on the sofa. "Julie, there was another girl in the secretarial pool at Colby…"

"I'm not in the pool. I have my own desk. You saw it."

"I did. You and Ms. Stern seem to have floated to the top."

"Top of what?"

"The secretarial pool."

She thought about that, then smiled. "You're kind of funny, aren't you?"

"Some people think I'm hilarious."

"Mark me one of 'em. You mean Vickie Dorn."

"Victoria Dorn, yeah. She was killed a while back."

She drew in breath through her nose, let it out the same way. "That was awful. Strangled or something. And raped. Raped first, I suppose."

"Right. Didn't Vincent date her?"

She shrugged and shook her head simultaneously. "He went

out with her a few times. I don't think it got serious. They weren't a…thing. Not that I know of, anyway."

"Were you friends with Vickie?"

"Work friends."

"Did she say anything about Vincent?"

The big blue eyes got narrow. "You mean, like…did he like it rough?"

"Right. Like did he like it rough?"

She shrugged. "I didn't know Vickie that well. But if Vincent likes it rough, *wouldn't* I know? From Sheila? We *are* friends, not just work friends."

I gestured around us. "Friends before you got this place together?"

"Work friends till then. Better friends now."

I frowned. "I didn't know Sheila ever worked at Colby's."

"She didn't. We used to waitress together at Café Reggio's. When I got the job at Colby's, we could afford this place. She'd stop by there sometimes and that's when Vincent saw her and, you know, liked what he saw."

"Kind of pursued her, you mean."

"No. He was just friendly. Flirted some, but…you need to talk to Sheila about that."

"Got it."

"I didn't mean to get snippy."

"You didn't get snippy at all, Julie. I'm just a snoop. It's what they pay me for."

Her smile was cuter than a box of puppies. "Yeah. You're a detective. Like Magnum. You sure you don't want a beer or a wine cooler?"

"No, I'm fine." I patted her arm. "Listen, honey...sorry about all the questions. And you don't have to keep me company or anything. You don't have to entertain me."

Another shrug. "I don't mind."

I glanced toward the door. "I thought Sheila was going to be here soon."

"Could take her a while. Do you know what daddy issues are?"

I gestured to the coffee table. "*Field and Stream*?"

Her gaze got pointed. "It means I have a thing for older guys. Not just *any* guys. Just certain ones. A certain...type."

She wiggled her eyebrows at me.

I said, "Uh, look, Julie...I'm old enough to be your father."

"But you *aren't* my father. Did I mention he was a policeman?"

This was every kind of wrong all at once.

I shifted on the couch again. "If you want to hump your old man, baby, don't tell *me* about it. Find yourself a shrink. Maybe find one under forty."

That made her laugh a little. She stood. She shrugged as she tugged at the silk belt and that's all it took for that dressing gown to slide down her smooth skin and puddle at her feet.

Her flesh was a creamy pale pink thing she wore with pride, her breasts neither small nor large but perfect, nipples erect within their puffy, darker pink settings, her waist tapering narrow then sweeping back out into full hips. She did a slow pirouette for me, proud of the rest of her flesh, too, the graceful back, the dimpled, rounded behind, which itself was an architectural marvel of uplift.

What was my secretary's name again?

Then she sat in Daddy's lap, where she was able to confirm her effect on me, and her arms went around my neck and then her mouth was on mine, warm and moist…

"Ten years ago," I whispered into the sweet, naughty face, "what a wild time we'd have had. But, darling child, I have a woman at home." Named Velda. "And you need to be more careful about who you share your riches with."

"I have rubbers," she said.

The bluntness of that wilted the moment, among other things, and I lifted the kid by the narrow waist and set her down next to me.

"Put your robe on," I said crankily.

She looked embarrassed now, as if Daddy had scolded her, and she scooped the silk thing off the floor and went padding into the bathroom in the nearby hall, fanny jiggling. Somebody needed to paddle that kid.

But not me.

I was chuckling to myself, shaking my head, when the front door opened, and my first reaction was to think of what Sheila Ryan might have walked into.

But maybe she wouldn't even have noticed an old man banging a young girl, because Sheila Ryan was crying, hysterical as hell, screaming, "Gino! *Gino!*"

I went over to her and took her gently by the forearms. "He's not here."

Her eyes were wide and wet. "I *know* he's not here! …What are *you* doing here, Mr. Hammer?"

Then she shook her head and pushed me away, saying, "*What does it matter!* He's dead! Gino is *dead!*"

CHAPTER ELEVEN

NoHo—the area north of Houston Street, with its quiet tree-lined streets, early 19th-century homes, and former factories with cast-iron facades—had been turning trendy for a while now. Three main arteries and small, sometimes cobblestone side streets hosted boutiques, eateries, art galleries and avant-garde theaters. Artistic types and Yuppies had discovered the neighborhood a while ago, but the tourists hadn't gotten wise. You didn't have to be rich—not yet anyway—to live in a loft-like pad in a former dry-goods warehouse like this one.

You could also die here.

Just ask Gino Mazzini.

He was where I'd found him, a corpse in his jockey shorts leaning against a wall of the sparsely furnished apartment, his legs akimbo, forming a V that pointed to the rest of him, his head so slumped he might have broken his neck trying to fellate himself.

But he was a casualty of something even nastier: the now-familiar cannonball blow to the chest, which had driven his blue-and-red Mets 1986 World Series t-shirt into him like a line drive with a bowling ball. He'd been killed at least three or four hours ago, because this stiff was stiff all right—rigor mortis had set in.

The mist had kept its promise, though the thunder had overstated its case, raindrops half-heartedly spattering, then angling down the slanted glass like unattended tears, throwing eerie shadow streaks on a room lighted only by a bedside lamp. It was half an hour or so past my discovery of the body, which I'd made with a key and directions from Sheila Ryan, who'd remained with her friend Julie.

Seemed when she'd got there to collect her things, Sheila had knocked, no answer, then used her key to get in. She found her ex-boyfriend dead, with his chest pushed in. That's all I bothered to get from her before heading to the bartender's NoHo loft apartment—Pat would get the details out of her later.

The apartment was mostly one big room, dominated by a king bed with black faux-silk sheets and a few cheap black-and-white modern furnishings from one of those "apartment living" joints; a fridge hummed in the kitchenette, its overhead light the only other illumination, and the john was boxed in at a corner (I checked, but no corpse was seated in there this time).

The gray walls were bare but for a pair of framed movie posters—*Rocky*, signed "Best," with a fluid scrawl that presumably said, "Sylvester Stallone," and *The Godfather Part II* autographed to the late tenant by Robert DeNiro ("You mix a mean Martini!").

Pat Chambers, glancing at the posters with a humorless smirk, said, "Well, at least he was proud of his heritage."

We stood there in our trenchcoats and snapbrim hats, daring the rain to get at us, two men from another time, staring at a man totally out of time. The forensics team hadn't arrived yet, but one uniform was on the landing outside and another at the bottom of the stairs at the street.

The captain of the Homicide Division worked days, of course, but I'd called him at home, knowing if I didn't somebody else would. Everybody at the PD knew who among the brass was personally handling the murders that the newspapers had not realized constituted a single story yet, since the small detail of victims with caved-in chests continued to be withheld.

"This *will* get out," I said. "Four kills with the same distinctive MO. Four kills tied to each other in various ways."

"Jasmine Jordan isn't."

He was staring at the dead man. We were maybe four feet from the body's bare feet.

"Not yet she isn't," I said. "But three victims definitely are— Kraft, Shannon, and now the Italian Stallion here. And you and I both know the Jordan broad is somewhere in the mix."

Neither of us said anything for a while.

Rather dryly, Pat commented, "The papers will say we have a serial killer on the loose. Another Son of Sam."

"Will they be wrong?" I gestured at the flesh-and-blood pile of evidence before us. "Just because some thread connects the murders doesn't make this less the act of a homicidal maniac."

His laugh was short and had little to do with the normal reasons for laughter. "The FBI would disagree with you. They define a serial killer as someone who commits at least three murders over more than a month…with an emotional cooling off period in between. No traditional motive but a deviant sexual aspect."

"You say tomato."

The gray-blue eyes looked at me now. "Mass murderer is closer. Anyway, who are you to talk? You make Jack the Ripper look like a piker."

"Hey, I'm just a good citizen, helping keep the city clean." I shrugged. "So he's not a serial killer, technically – but he *is* a cold-blooded bastard, removing people who know too much about him."

Those eyes narrowed. "You mean, your client. Vincent Colby."

"He's not my client, his father is." I started counting off on my fingers. "Shannon was zeroing in on young Colby for the strangled secretary and the hit-and-run boiler-room broker. That dominatrix kept a little black book with her clients in it, and if she wasn't blackmailing a certain one, who liked to dish it out rough—and if his name wasn't Vincent Colby, whose favorite room at the Tube is the S & M suite, then I'm in the wrong damn business. As for our dead mixologist here, he was the previous boy friend of Vincent's current squeeze—a young female that Vincent is obsessive about, who the ex here liked to pound like minute steak."

He was nodding, barely. "The girl who found the body."

"Sheila Ryan, yeah. You'll be talking to her. Tonight, I bet."

Another non-laugh. "How smart you are. But smart enough to explain the *second* hit-and-run? The one that clipped young Colby right in front of your private eyes?"

I thought for a moment, then shrugged again. "Could be Colby and Kraft had a prior grudge. Maybe Colby's been backing the play of that bank-heisting crew. Maybe he staked them and was getting a cut of the action, and the crew got more successful than they ever dreamed of and Kraft was sent out to get rid of a troublesome ongoing expense."

"Oh brother." His eyes rolled. "You are *really* reaching."

I leaned in and thumped his chest with a forefinger. "Or maybe Kraft was hired to do that first hit-and-run in the parking ramp! Maybe for some reason Vincent Colby wanted that broker dead and hired a hit, and then stiffed Kraft or otherwise had a falling out with him. So Kraft tried to run *him* down, too."

He was shaking his head. "Sad. Really sad to see the depths a once great deductive mind has sunk to."

It was time to throw my hands in the air, so I did. "Okay, so our killer isn't a textbook serial. He isn't a mass murderer by standard thinking, either. Neither was Penta—*he* was a hit man who left a serial-killer-style signature."

"Granted."

"But for some reason, somebody—and it looks like Vincent Colby to me, just about *has* to be Vincent Colby—is settling old scores or cleaning up after himself. Right now we can see no connective tissue between the kills, other than Colby *himself*— he's the connective tissue. Colby, who has martial arts training. Colby, who has outbursts of rage since his concussion. And all of these *bunkai* kills, remember, came after Vincent got hit by that car."

Silence.

Then, finally, Pat said, "I don't disagree."

"Good. Nice to see *your* great deductive mind hasn't sunk."

His eyes returned to mine. "I'm making no deductions yet. Not necessary. Simply experiencing the resistance any good cop has to coincidence. A resistance a certain Michael Hammer claims never to have had."

"No resistance, buddy," I said, "when there are *this* many coincidences."

The forensics team arrived and Pat gave them some instructions, then he sent me home. I offered to sit in on the Ryan girl's interview, but he said no. He was still going this one alone, and I, if anybody, understood the impulse.

I had called Velda to say I'd be late. She met me at her door, hair freshly washed, all that creamy skin smelling of soap and wrapped up in a pink chiffon robe that hugged her figure in a way that made that Julie Olsen kid look sick. Of course, that kid *was* sick with that daddy complex of hers.

With it going on two a.m., I suggested we go down to the all-night diner for a breakfast that was either very early or really damn late; but she cooked me some eggs and bacon herself, instead. I risked a cup of coffee because I didn't think there was enough caffeine in the world to threaten my tiredness at the end of this interminable day.

So I filled her in about the new murder—all that got was wide eyes and a shake of the head out of her—and recapped my conversation with Pat.

She sat down with her own plate of just one scrambled egg and a cup of coffee, incredibly beautiful without a bit of make-up, and said, "You really think that's what's going on?"

"It's got Vincent Colby written all over it, doll. He's gone psycho after the head injury, and he's going after a laundry list of people who crossed him or offended him. The trouble is, unless

Pat gets lucky with a witness who saw him at one of the scenes, or some other standard perp failing…each one of these murders has to be individually looked at, because the motives are singular."

An eyebrow went up. "This doesn't seem like a perp with many if any failings."

"I did keep one thing from Pat."

"Oh?"

"He doesn't know about Chris Peters and me making that trip to Shannon's place, or the floppy disk we found. Poor ol' Patrick would have a cow. So my sniffing Obsession on my attacker I kept to myself, too."

She smiled wryly over the rim of her coffee cup. "Popular cologne, Mike. Narrows your suspect list to a few hundred thousand New York males. Not your usual mystery, is it, darling?"

"What do you mean?"

She made a cute face. "No whodunit with a big surprise at the end."

"You never know. I may come up with a big surprise for this prick yet."

The phone rang—always a startling thing in the wee hours. She took the kitchen extension on the wall nearby.

"Yes…yes, Pat…Well, he's right here…Oh. Oh, okay…All right, I'll tell him."

She hung up. Her expression was dazed.

"What?" I asked.

"Pat interviewed Sheila Ryan," Velda said, and sat back down. She was looking past me, into thoughts that were forming. "Sheila was with Vincent Colby earlier this evening—*all* evening."

I set my cup down, sloshingly. "Is Pat *sure*? She was at that Olsen girl's apartment earlier, I thought."

"No, that was later. Exact time of death is yet to be determined, remember, but rigor had set in…"

"So when Sheila found Gino," I said, my words in slow motion, "he had been dead at least three or four hours."

Her eyes narrowed to slits. "Mike…if Vincent Colby didn't kill that bartender, then somebody is fitting our client's kid for a frame—elaborate enough to fool Mike Hammer."

"Maybe," I said. "Maybe."

Gansevoort Street – running east to west in downtown Manhattan's riverfront neighborhood, till the Hudson cut it rudely off— undulated its cobblestone way along the foot of the brick warehouses known as the Meatpacking District. Here animal carcasses began their travel to the kitchens of Manhattan restaurants and residences from considerately distant slaughterhouses. Little had changed for decades in this foreboding, desolate-looking section of the city, though a few galleries and eateries had started popping up, like stubborn mushrooms, to foretell a fashionable future. On this sunshiny but chill November afternoon, a red-trimmed black 1985 Ford Mustang LX pulled out from in front of a warehouse onto an all but deserted Gansevoort. The driver immediately hit the gas, really punching it with a clear straightaway ahead.

Clear, anyway, till a dark green Mercury Capri emerged from an alley and into the Mustang's path.

Honking his displeasure, the driver swerved around the

Mercury, just missing collision, but before any sense of relief came, a mother in jeans and a parka came out from between parked cars, jaywalking a baby in its stroller right in front of the oncoming Mustang.

With a screech of brakes, the red-and-black vehicle wheeled around the obstacle, the woman helping avoid tragedy by running, the cobblestone street giving the stroller and its contents a rough ride, but safely out of harm's way.

All well and good, but the driver in the Mustang now confronted two town cars coming right at him, taking up both lanes of the one-way street, and he could only avoid them by riding up on the sidewalk, sending a few random pedestrians scurrying.

Swinging back into the street now, the Mustang and its driver were confronted by a pile of construction materials beyond which were heaps of sand. The former acted as a ramp, overturning the vehicle and returning it to the street upside-down, the latter stirring up a hazy cloud to makes things even worse.

The Mustang skidded down the street on its roof, like a turtle some cruel child had uncaringly tossed. It came to a spinning stop, finally, but its tires continued on their ride to nowhere.

"*Cut!*"

The B-unit director, a guy in his thirties in an NYPD baseball cap, Yankees t-shirt and sweats, turned to a clutch of waiting crew members. "*Go!* Get over there!"

Three guys in sweatshirts and jeans scurried to help the driver out of the turned-over car. Four 35mm cameras, at strategic locations, including one riding train-like tracks and another on a crane with a jib, had captured the elaborate stunt, which had seemed to be the work of a major male star behind the wheel. You'd recognize him.

But as soon as he got his feet under him, the driver yanked off the rubber mask resembling that famous white actor—who was watching from the sidelines, smiling, chewing gum—and revealed himself as my African-American friend Thalmus Lockhart who was stunt and special effects coordinator on the film.

Velda and I were sightseers, approved in advance thanks to Thalmus. I just couldn't seem to get away from warehouses and cobblestones.

Thal spotted Velda and me, on the sidelines, and grinned and nodded and waved, then took off Caucasian-colored gloves and handed them to a crew member.

The B-unit director yelled, "Okay, next set-up! Warehouse rumble! Check your bullet hits and blood bags, boys!"

My friend—a muscular six-footer with a shaved head and a close-trimmed horseshoe mustache—came trotting over to us in a yellow turtleneck, jeans and running shoes. This side of the street had been off-camera, lined as it was with Ryder rental trucks, Winnebagos, honeywagons (semi-trailers of portable toilets), massive lights and craft service (snack) tables.

We shook hands and exchanged grins.

"When *I* drive like that," I said, "I get my ass in stir or the hospital or both."

"When I do," Thal said, "I get paid. You want to say hello to Burt?"

"Why not?"

"Well, he may be grouchy. He hates not doing his own stunts."

Velda and I went over and met the star of the film, who was dressed identically to Thal. But the actor (and former stunt man) was not grouchy at all, and flashed his trademark smile at Velda, who could compete with any actress Hollywood threw at him. The guy could barely keep his eyes off her, and who could blame him?

After a brief jokey chat with movie royalty, Thal took us inside the warehouse and over to a craft service table in a corner. The lighting was being tweaked on much of the yawning space nearby with its iron catwalks and brick walls. We helped ourselves to coffee and a cookie or two before the stunt coordinator showed us to waiting director's chairs with GUEST on the canvas backing; we sat, Velda in the middle, out of the path of the bustling, buzzing movie set.

Thal, as a stunt coordinator, did many of his own gags—as movie folk called stunts and on-set "practical" special effects. About forty, he'd made a splash in the early seventies as Richard Roundtree's stunt double. He was expert at non-stunt effects, too, such as horror make-up and prosthetic masks like the one he'd worn today. But his specialty was stunt driver.

"Mike, my man," he said. "I only have a few minutes. Big scene coming up. But you can hang till after, if you like."

Thal nodded toward the set, where much of the warehouse was now bathed in moody lighting. A young woman in torn clothing and carefully mussed hair, center stage, was tied into a chair with a shaft of light singling her out. A make-up woman was applying smudges to the face of the actress, who was frowning in concentration. She'd been in a couple of movies lately, good roles.

Thal said, "I have to help Burt rescue that little Satan's spawn."

Velda asked, "That's what she's playing? Is this an *Exorcist* movie or something?"

"No. She's just an awful person. What can I do for you two?"

I said, "Did you ever work with a guy named Roger Kraft?"

Thal's eyes tightened and he grunted, then nodded. "I saw in the *News* that somebody murdered that crumb bum. Sorry to speak ill of the dead."

"Feel free," I said.

He shifted in the canvas-and-wood chair. "Yeah, I did work with the S.O.B. a few times. He was good—very little he couldn't do as a driver, and he had mechanical know-how, too. But he was *baaaaad* news."

"How so?"

"He took too many risks, always cowboying up. Sometimes that's what the job calls for, and the combat pay justifies. But you learn pretty quick this trade is about safety, not thrills. About helping tell an exciting story, y'know? Also, he was a fuckin' liar… pardon the language, Velda."

She smiled. "An f-bomb drops around the office occasionally."

I asked, "A liar how, Thal?"

"Well, I was stunt coordinator on those *Shaft* TV movies, a while back. First time in my career I was more than just a guy doing gags. A series is an ongoing gig and you have would-be hires fill out applications like on any job. He lied on his. He'd been in the joint for armed robbery, turns out."

"You wouldn't have hired him, if you'd known?"

That made a face. "That's not it—I would have given him a

break. Stunt men are a mixed bag—they're all a little crazy. Ex-bouncers, circus acrobats, wing-walkers, cowboys…I mean, *real* cowboys…all types, and that includes ex-cons. Anybody who's done his time, I'm fine with givin' a second chance. But I do not like to be, excuse me, fucking lied to."

"Thal," I said, "let me tell you about a hit-and-run I witnessed recently."

And I went into what happened outside Pete's Chophouse, including the sense I'd had about it that something just didn't feel right.

As I wrapped it up, I said, "Could that have been faked?"

His frown was thoughtful. "You mean, could Kraft have hit that guy just right and not hurt him? Not unless they were both in on it."

Velda gave me a sharp look.

I said, "What if they were? For example…is that a stunt you could stage for a flick?"

His laugh was big. "Oh, hell yes. Easy peasy. But you'd have to be a pro…both of ya, not just the driver."

"A talented amateur couldn't pull off the victim role? Somebody with martial arts training and an athletic background? Former college athlete, maybe?"

He shook his head. "Probably not without some special training. Some real practice. Likely some padding under the clothes too. In that case…doable."

Velda and I exchanged glances.

I said, "Can you think of anybody locally who might be up for that? A trainer who thought he was getting somebody ready for a movie stunt...or just didn't give a shit how his training got used?"

This laugh wasn't so big. "I know *exactly* the guy."

I blinked. "You're kidding. How can you be so sure? Zero in right away like that?"

"Because you've been asking me about that Kraft dude, Michael my man, and this is a guy who knew Kraft, who worked with him, both hand-to-hand stuff and stunt driving. I fired both their asses off that *Shaft* shoot."

Velda got out her notebook and took down the name—Harry Strutt.

"No idea," he told her, "what address. And whether he's even still around town. But if he is? He'd be the natural one to work with Kraft on somethin' shady." He winked at her. "Maybe you can find a detective who can track him down."

"Maybe," Velda said.

A pretty young woman in a baseball hat, NYU t-shirt, and jeans with a clipboard in her hands came up to Thal and said, "You're needed, Mr. Lockhart."

"Thank you, Sal."

She went off, providing sweet rear view.

Thal asked me, "You know what she's paid?"

"Not enough," I said.

Velda elbowed me.

"Not a red cent," Thal said. "She's what you call a production assistant. An intern, college kid. Does more work than any salaried man on the picture."

Velda said, "I know the feeling."

Thal stood and so did we.

The stuntman stuck out his paw and I shook it.

"Listen, Mike," he said, settling a hand on my shoulder, "you ever need anything, you know where to come. Just say the word and I'm there. That was one hell of a jam you got me out of."

Couple years back, he'd been in a bar fight in which a guy had died. I had found the other two guys involved and proved one of them had delivered the killing blows. Thal had nixed the heavy drinking after I cleared him. Win–win.

We stayed around to watch the little Satan's spawn gal get rescued a couple of times. Thal fought the six bad guys holding her; shot two of them, went martial arts on the asses of the other four. One knocked Thal behind a crate, but it was Burt who came out from behind it to untie the distressed damsel.

She was grateful, till the director called, "Cut."

CHAPTER TWELVE

Years ago, when Velda went missing and I was on the hunt, I had headed out to find an upstate farmhouse where she might be held. The only difference this time was the daylight I was driving in, though the grayness overhead all but cancelled that out, the rain coming right at me at a discouraging slant, my wipers working overtime.

At the office, Velda had gathered some info for me from a policewoman contact. A mugshot of Harold D. Strutt, 38, was faxed over to us and gave us what's what on our man. Strutt had done two terms at Sing Sing, one for armed robbery, another for breaking and entering; several arrests on various charges had not been brought to trial. He was twice divorced with three kids and had been flagged as a deadbeat dad.

I turned off Palisades Drive and caught the Throughway, my Ford heap plowing through rain for over an hour before I swung off again, taking 17K into Newburgh. I went on to Marlboro before stopping outside the city limits at a filling station to ask the way to Harry Strutt's farmhouse.

The attendant was young and had no idea, but he yelled at an older guy who might know, who came over to give me directions.

He had a deeply grooved face and white hair with a burr haircut, and I just knew he was ex-military, the right age for my war. I wondered what hell he'd gone through only to wind up pumping gas and checking oil. Or maybe he owned the place, and the American dream had worked out for him.

He was looking at me funny, a warrior's nasty grin in that wrinkled puss. "What do you want with Strutt?"

"It's your business?"

"No. No. It's just…he's awful popular today, for somebody that nobody around here cares for much."

"Why's that?"

"He's a drinker and a bragger and he gets into fights just for the hell of it."

"You don't say."

His nod was slow. "He's no farmer. Just been rentin' out that way, last year or so. If you're his friend, I mean no offense. If you're lookin' for him for your own reasons…I just figured you might like the skinny."

That seemed a funny thing for him to say. Then he said something not funny at all.

"You know, you're the third…*interestin'* feller who stopped here to ask directions out to Strutt's today."

I chuckled. "By 'interesting' you wouldn't happen to mean 'lowlife,' by any chance?"

His white gas-station uniform was as crisp as his smile was rumpled; both he and his jumpsuit were protected by the canopy over the pumps.

"I recognize you from the papers, Hammer. You're no lowlife. What I would call the boys who stopped for directions…each in his own vehicle over a kinda staggered bit of time today…is hardcases."

"Like me?"

His grinned was stained. "I don't think any other hardcase is quite like you, Hammer. Should I check the paper out tomorrow, you think?"

"Maybe. But sometimes interesting stories fall through the cracks."

"Like interestin' fellers do?"

"Like interesting fellers do…sometimes. If I handed you a five-spot, would you be offended?"

"Damn straight I would. I'm the owner. I catch any of my help takin' a tip, I kick 'em in the ass."

"I bet you do." I gave him a little salute, which he returned with that rumpled smile, and pulled into the rain, which was getting more insistent.

The third farmhouse after I took the blacktop into the country had the STRUTT mailbox. Neighbors seemed spaced pretty far apart out here. I slowed a little for a look. A silo and a barn indicated somebody was farming this land, though apparently not the rental resident of the big, rambling, ramshackle house, white faded to gray. A long gravel drive bordered on one side by trees and on the other by indifferently tended grass widened into an apron, where four cars were parked close to a covered front porch.

I drove perhaps half a mile before tucking the Ford into a cornfield's access, rows of dried brown stalk stumps dripping and leaves shuddering under what was now a near downpour.

For a while, I just sat there. The rain drummed on the roof of the car, steadily, like a drum and bugle corps minus the horns. Thunder would rumble, then roar, and lightning would light up the cornfield, where those leaves seemed to shiver in fear.

What was going on back there?

What could *be going on?*

My hunch was that Harry Strutt was part of that bank robbery crew, and this was a planning session. But the hardcases who stopped one at a time at that filling station had needed to find out how to get to Strutt's. Curiouser and curiouser, somebody said.

If Strutt was part of the heist crew, why did they need directions to his place?

What if, now that Kraft was on a morgue slab, they needed a new driver, and Kraft's pal Strutt had been elected? Thal Lockhart had indicated Strutt was a stunt driver, too.

The rain kept up its rhythm and I just sat there wondering whether to dance or go home. Come back another time, maybe. Or sit it out and wait till Strutt's guests took their leave...

After all, the bank heist crew, if that's who these cars belonged to, was not the point of my country sojourn—talking to *Strutt* was; the goal was getting him to own up to training Vincent Colby for that hit-and-run farce.

What did rounding up some (presumed) bank robbers have to do with the job at hand? Not a damn thing.

But I was an officer of the court, wasn't I? Didn't I have a responsibility to check this out and, if my assumptions about them were right, haul their sorry asses in?

Still, I sat there for maybe fifteen minutes sorting through my several shitty options, waiting for the rain to let up, which it never did. I prepared to brave the storm. Should I ditch the raincoat, to give myself more freedom of movement, and maybe leave the porkpie fedora on, to keep at least a little of the rain off me? Out of my eyes, anyway?

But I left the raincoat on, and of course the hat, with the brim down all the way round, and walked down the blacktop with my 1911 Colt .45 in my right-hand raincoat pocket, my left hand gathering the lapels of the coat as tight and protective as I could manage. The only break I got from God or nature or somebody was that I wasn't walking straight into the rain—it was at my back, and actually seemed to be prodding me, pushing me along.

When I turned down the gravel lane, I veered off along the tree line. That sheltered me somewhat from the downpour, and from getting much water in my eyes for that matter. A whipcrack of lightning would occasionally light the landscape up in momentary white.

When I got closer, I saw that the cars were recent models, their beautiful paint jobs pearled with raindrops—a Chrysler Conquest, a Corvette, a Mustang GT, a Firebird. Parked alongside the house was an older model Camaro – Strutt's ride, probably.

This might mean the veteran thieves, with their successful run of bank knockovers, were spending money like they won the lottery. On the other hand, the vintage car might indicate Strutt wasn't part of the crew yet, or at least was its newest member—driving a Camaro ten years older than these '88 models his visitors had arrived in.

At the end of the stand of trees, I paused, my left hand still clutching the raincoat collars tight, wondering what my next move should be.

Knock?

And when Strutt answered the door, with his guests hiding out somewhere, upstairs maybe, give the guy a story and talk myself inside? But Harry just might recognize his unexpected guest—from my notoriety in the media, or maybe knowing I was involved in the Vincent Colby affair. I was the guy who found his pal Roger Kraft's body, after all.

Or, hell—when he answered, I could just shoulder in with my gun, ready for whatever might happen!

Neither was much of a plan. Strutt could come to the door with a gun at the ready himself, and his guests could be nearby, also armed and poised to respond. I would never get across the threshold without assembling an impressive collection of slugs of various calibers in assorted locations in my body.

The sun was up there somewhere, but you'd never know it, the growly grayness invaded by swarming black clouds turning late afternoon into near midnight. And the yellow glow from the windows said the lights were only on toward the front of the house, and along one window on this side of the house, at the rear.

I did some recon.

Moving quickly, staying low, hugging the house as best as I could, keeping below the windows, I made my way around the entire structure. Finally I sneaked up onto the typical farmhouse front porch, happy to get out of the rain. The windows were tall with curtains that didn't quite meet, allowing me to peek in.

The living room was sparsely furnished in a bachelor pad style not suited to the age of the house or its somewhat rundown condition. An overhead light fixture was dim, and an end table lamp didn't add much. Riding a wall was a velvet painting based on a *Playboy* centerfold, and hugging that same wall was a projection TV.

No humans present, not even loosely defined.

The only illumination elsewhere was in the kitchen—from a window alongside the rear of the house I could get a low view, looking up, of some appliances and cupboards. And I could hear talk in there, normal levels of speech made murmurs by the pounding rain and occasional thunder. Taking off my hat, I risked standing on tiptoe and doing the window-peeking bit for a few seconds, getting a quick but complete eyeful before ducking back down.

Slamming the porkpie back on, wiping the rain rivulets from my face, I took stock of what I'd seen.

Five men were seated at a round table in a cramped kitchen, including the host, who looked older than his mugshot—though his back was to me, he was talking to the guy next to him. Strutt had dark hair with a pony tail and a scruffy beard, and wore a black wife-beater t-shirt that showed off muscle-builder biceps.

Next to Harry was a medium-size, mustached, hair-gelled guy who thought he was handsome and was wrong, decked out in a green sweater vest, pointy-collared blue shirt and a floral thing that was a scarf suffering under the delusion that it was a tie.

Next door was a skinny, balding, droopily mustached guy, in a well-worn denim jacket and shiny yellow shirt. He had only the barest excuse for a chin. He was smoking a cigarette.

Beside him sat an older guy, tiny-eyed and sporting a Moe Howard haircut, a little heavy, in a suit and tie—probably the leader. Or maybe the Moe resemblance made me assume that. He was smoking, too—a cheroot.

Next, and to my far left as I'd peeked in, was a big burly guy who was obviously the muscle, a blunt-featured butch-haircut dope who was going *Miami Vice* with a pink jacket over a pastel blue t-shirt that said, you guessed it, *Miami Vice*.

Spread out before them like a not-quite-big-enough tablecloth was a large hand-drawn map in magic marker. I couldn't be sure from the gander I got, but I would bet it was of the layout of a bank.

That was the heist crew, all right.

I risked popping up for another look and got more confirmation.

The not-handsome guy had a .38 in front of him near a bottle of Hamm's, the denim jacket chinless guy had a nine mil near a can of Bud and an ashtray, the Moe haircut bozo a .22 Ruger by a coffee cup, and the *Miami Vice* dope, who was drinking a Diet Coke, had a leather strap running under prominent pecs that indicated a shoulder holster.

A lot of firepower.

But nobody knew I was here, and a .45 held eight rounds—of course, I only loaded in seven these days, since Velda insisted that resting the hammer on a live round is a really bad idea. With five men at that table, that still gave a spare two rounds…and an extra clip in my left-hand pocket.

Four steps led up to the back door, which opened right onto the kitchen. If it unlocked, I'd be in good shape. I could walk right in and say hello. But if it was locked, I just might wind up dead.

So I considered alternate ways in.

They say it's better to be lucky than smart, and I was lucky enough to discover that the storm cellar doors were unlocked. I opened one side and slipped in, shut it behind me and then lingered on the wooden steps. Sat on one briefly. I got my mini-Maglite out and had a look around the cellar. Not much of anything—it was a hard dirt floor and not great for storage, but there were a few boxes anyway. A beat-up washer and drier. A furnace dating to the Eisenhower administration.

Also stairs that seemed positioned to open onto or near the kitchen.

I abandoned the sopped hat to the dirt floor, the raincoat, too.

Soon I was heading up those stairs, my trusty gum soles on the old wooden stairs making very little noise—no more creaks and squeaks than the average mouse, and anyway it was probably rats down here.

And above.

With my Maglite switched off and tucked away, the .45 in my fist led the way. When I got to the top step, I was breathing a little hard—not fatigue, adrenalin—and I paused to get my bearings and listen.

I could hear them talking, clear as if they were on the other side of this door, which they were. No idea which voice belonged to who, but the gist of their conversation made itself clear immediately.

"The guard's over sixty, easily."

My guess was this was Moe, the leader, his voice resonant, dripping leadership.

Someone else said, "A retired cop, probably."

The leader again: "Probably. That means nothing, really."

As I listened, he would speak and another of the crew would respond and then he would speak again.

The resonant voice continued: "Stick a gun in his face, take his weapon, push him to the floor."

"They close at two?"

"They close at two. We go in ten minutes before that, diddle around making out deposit slips and such, wait for any other customers to leave. Probably someone will politely tell us the bank is closing, and that's our cue. You each know your jobs. No shooting unless necessary. Harry, did you scope things out?"

"Yeah. Yellow curb in front of the bank, but plenty of parking places on either side of it. I'll park the car first thing, close as I can. Go back to my hotel room half a block away, and feed the meter all day. Then around one-thirty, I'll get in the car and I'll be there waiting for you, motor running, when you come out. And we will haul ass."

"Perfect."

"Hey, it's my first job with you boys, but it ain't my first time at the rodeo."

"I bet it isn't."

Judging by their voices, as I stood on the top step with the .45 in one hand and the door knob in the other, that table would be *right there* when I burst in. Of course, the door might be locked, but that seemed unlikely. Why would anyone lock the basement door? Unless it was to keep someone out who broke in that way...

You know – like me.

But if Strutt was that cautious, those storm doors wouldn't have been left unlocked. Right?

Right?

Still, if this door turned out to be locked, or just stuck because the wood had warped or whatever, I would have to shoulder my way in, putting some real muscle into it...else face a very well-armed welcoming committee...

I thought about what I would say.

"Hands high, fellas—you're under arrest!" Corny but appropriate. I could always add, "The place is surrounded." Another old favorite, if a lie.

The door wasn't locked and I went in quick.

The table of thieves was only a few feet away, and their faces were on me like a lynch mob. I was about to get my prepared words out when Strutt, his frown squeezing in on itself so hard it hurt to look at it, yelled: *"Hammer!"*

I can't tell you whether he had warned them about my involvement in the convoluted affair that had cost their driver Kraft his life. Or if this select group just knew me because we were, in a way, in the same business, and mine was a famous face in these kinds of circles. Or if they just read in that one outburst from Strutt a mélange of anger merged with fear underscored by surprise.

In any event, they went for their guns, three of them for the weapons on the table, and the big muscle guy for a rod in his shoulder holster under the Don Johnson jacket.

The quarters could have hardly been any closer, and my only advantage was having my gun already in hand.

It was enough.

I took them clockwise starting with the not-handsome guy, whose head came apart in chunks, like a target-range cantaloupe. The chinless guy in the denim jacket got his in the side of the head and I could see his eyes go blank as much of his brain sprayed out of his opposite temple and splattered a nearby refrigerator with bloody gray goop. Next, closest to me, came the brains of the outfit, who lost a good share of his when his neck swivelled to see me and a slug slammed through his forehead to splat its contents onto, then dripping down, a cupboard, like a great big bug that hit a windshield. The *Miami Vice* thug almost had his gun out when a .45 slug traveled through his throat and had him gurgling and thrashing, until my second shot, piercing his thick forehead this time, ended his suffering.

The 1911 Colt .45 is a single-action pistol — you cock the hammer before each shot — and the trigger has a short reset. The four bank robbers had died in that many seconds. Strutt might have been a problem, but the indoor thunder of the .45 and the carnage and flying gore had spooked him, and his startled rabbit expression accompanied a hand that hovered over a .38 Police Special but didn't touch it.

The cordite-filled air was making my eyes burn. I pointed the .45 at him and he raised his hands and was crying. Maybe the cordite. Maybe not.

"This is unpleasant in here," I said. "I think a couple of these guys shit themselves. Let's go in the living room where it's quiet and maybe light a scented candle or something. We need to talk."

I gestured with the .45 and he swallowed, wiping his tears away with a forearm, and headed glumly into the nearby living room. I could see now that his wife-beater t-shirt had four aces and a pair of dice on it; his jeans were worn and so were his tennies.

With the snout of the weapon I indicated a black overstuffed fake-leather sofa and he sat. I settled into an adjacent matching armchair. On a low-slung coffee table were some scattered girlie magazines—*Caper, Escapade, Dude, Swank*. Maybe he had mommy issues.

"Jesus, man," he said. He looked sick. "You killed everybody."

"Not yet," I reminded him.

He swallowed. Absently, he scratched a bearded cheek. "What do you want from me?"

"The truth."

"About what the fuck?"

"About you and Vincent Colby."

"What truth is that, man?"

"You trained him for that stunt, Harry. Maybe you didn't know what your buddy Kraft and his client had in mind—faking that hit-and-run 'accident.' Maybe you thought it was for a movie or something. Or some elaborate prank. I'm willing to give you the benefit of the doubt."

"No idea what you're talking about, man."

"You need to think this through. The kind of trouble you're in."

His lip curled back taking some mustache with it. "*You're* the one in trouble. Break in here and fuckin' *shoot* everybody! You're out of your freaking *mind*, Hammer!"

I raised my free hand. "First of all, your friends all had guns and were about to use them on me. Second, I'm a licensed private investigator in New York State and heard you fellas planning a robbery. I have nothing to fear from this. But you do."

He tried not to look alarmed. "What do I have to fear?"

"I'm going to guess your Wall Street pal Vincent has greased your palm but good. You may be figuring that rich-guy money's gonna just keep flowing. But think about it."

"*You* think about it."

"I have. I think about how Roger Kraft was on the payroll and got killed. I think about how a cop named Shannon looking into young Colby's homicidal ways got himself killed, too, and you know how much the cops love it when one of their own buys it."

"Nothing to do with me."

"A hooker blackmailing Colby got killed last night, and so did a bartender who beat up Vincent's girl. Anybody who crosses that Golden Boy is on the chopping block. All this went down within a few days. And you're likely next."

He sneered again. "More likely *you*, Hammer. And maybe Roger tried to blackmail Colby or some shit, and got what blackmailers get."

"Is that what happened?"

He raised his palms shoulder high. "Just sayin' what *might* be. I have *nothing* for you, Hammer. And I'm not afraid of you."

That was hard to buy, with the coppery smell of his associates' blood wafting in on cordite waves with just a hint of the fragrance of human excrement.

I said, "If the cops bag your ass, Harry, you won't be just some guy who trained a rich kid for a prank. You'll be an accomplice. Probably to murder."

His smile in the nest of beard was not convincing. "How do you figure, Hammer? Suppose that *was* a phony accident I helped along. That's no murder rap."

"Kraft getting his makes it felony murder, sonny boy." That was a little thin but I didn't think Harry here knew much about the finer points of the law. "And for sure you're obstructing justice in a murder investigation by not coming forward."

His eyes narrowed. "*That's* what you want. Me to come forward."

"That's what I want."

What Pat Chambers would want.

"Okay." He swallowed. "I'll do it."

I had lowered the .45 a little, while we talked, and that must have encouraged him, because he came forward, all right. He dove off that sofa and right at me, taking the chair back and me with it, then with one powerful hand grabbed me by the right wrist and shook the rod out of my grasp, sending it tumbling on the shag carpet. Meanwhile that chair hit the floor, hard, and powerful fists were at me, a right hand to the face, a left hand to the kidneys.

I pushed him off and to one side, onto the floor, then twisted to throw myself on top of him, giving him a knee in the balls and then a right to the nose, breaking it, and a left to the jaw, jarring it on its hinges. He was wincing with the pain only a groin blow can bring, but he was, after all, a stunt man and obviously a muscle builder, so his testicles were probably the size of peas anyway, thanks to steroids. In any case, he had the will and presence of mind to shove his right forearm into my chest with enough power to send me tumbling back.

Then he jumped on me like a wrestler in the ring only not

phony, and he was pinning me with a knee and strangling me with two powerful hands. For a moment I wondered if he was the killer with the deadly knee move, but he smelled like pot, not Obsession. Gasping, I caught his pony tail with one hand and jerked his head back while with the other I hit him in the side, and busted a couple ribs because their snap was unmistakable. He cried out and his hands loosened, and I head-butted his chin, which rocked him back, and he stumbled off me and got to his feet and put a little distance between us.

I was still down low and I threw a tackle into him and he went backward, hitting his head hard on the edge of the projection TV. His eyes rolled back and he slid down to the floor and lay in a pile of random bones and muscles in a bag of flesh. Very quiet, but for some dripping blood.

I bent over and checked his pulse. Both his wrist and neck.

Then I stood staring down at him, thinking about what to do. Thinking about my situation.

I had a phone call to make. It would take going to a gas station and making a call, but I would be back.

I wasn't done here.

CHAPTER THIRTEEN

The Meatpacking District on a Sunday night was dead, the businesses for which the area took its name shuttered till tomorrow, the weathered buildings wearing graffiti like scars. Refuse blew down the cobblestone street like tumbleweed except where slowed by fetid-surfaced puddles.

No inhabitants were showing themselves. Even the underground gay scene with its leather shops, bathhouses and notorious sex clubs (The Manhole, The Hellfire Club) were, like God Almighty, taking a day of rest or anyway a night of recuperation. The rain stopped yesterday but the sky was still a dirty gray, not ready to turn loose of the world below. The block where Velda and I had visited the bustling movie location was a sinister ghost town now, the production having moved on.

My farmhouse visit had been Friday and yesterday was a day of prep, for what I faced tonight. The only development on Saturday had been the press reporting that the Ulster County Sheriff's Department, operating on an anonymous tip, discovered four bodies in a farmhouse, carnage that appeared to be the result of a falling-out among thieves.

The spate of bank robberies in upstate New York was being tentatively tied to this event, according to unnamed sources within the PD, and the whereabouts of the rented farmhouse's occupant, Harold P. Strutt, were not known. Meanwhile, New York State Police were looking for Strutt, who had a criminal record and whose 1978 white Camaro's license number was included in the All Points Bulletin seeking him and it. Identification of the other fatalities was being withheld, but registration of vehicles at the property matched identification on the bodies of the shooting victims. No fingerprints were found at the scene other than those of the victims and the missing occupant.

Velda, reading the *Daily News* in her pink terrycloth robe at her kitchen table over a breakfast I'd cooked, gave me an arched eyebrow. "Sounds like you had fun last night. You got in at what...four?"

"What you don't know can't hurt you."

"Risk it."

So I filled her in. I hated making an accessory out of her, but it couldn't be helped—I would need her with me on the next phase of the job.

Nibbling at a naked slice of toast, she said, "Then it really *is* Vincent Colby who's our killer. It's not a frame job."

"Not a frame job, no."

She gestured with a crust, fairly insistently. "What I don't understand is...*why?* Does Silver Spoon get his kicks out of murder? Is he some uniquely twisted spin on the serial killer concept? And why would he stage his own hit-and-run?"

I shrugged as I chewed my toast with its butter and strawberry jam. Politely swallowed before saying, "There's method to his madness, doll. Vincent Colby worked out at that Yuppie gym with *sensei* Sakai, got himself fit and learned some moves. He trained with a stunt man until he knew just how to roll with that Ferrari's punch. No, he knew just what he was doing."

"Fine. But, damnit, Mike—again...*why?*"

I smiled; the jam was sweet. "I think I know. Won't be easy to prove, though."

"Since when do *you* need proof?"

"Since I promised Pat."

She nodded. "Yeah. Yeah, I get that. Casey Shannon was Pat's friend. And you owe the guy that much. So how do we make that happen?"

I told her.

Her eyes seemed to have forgotten how to blink. "That's a little *out there*, isn't it?"

"Open to suggestions."

She had none.

And she wasn't with me Sunday night, while I waited outside the warehouse where that little Satan's spawn actress got saved several times by a movie star named Burt. Me, I was in costume, trenchcoat and hat and .45 in its speed rig, ready for my starring role as a hardboiled dick. The rod had a fresh shiny new barrel, the old one tossed down a sewer, having left its signature all over the dead guests at that farmhouse.

The lonely, ugly street, with its puddled cobblestones and crumbling brick and filthy sidewalks, made the perfect setting— even in color, this was a black-and-white movie. The only sign of life besides the occasional scurrying rat were the lights of the Florent a few blocks down, a coffee shop with great burgers and zany drag waitresses and a clientele out of Fellini.

A cab rolled up and its passenger climbed out with easy confidence. Vincent Colby—in a black silk t-shirt, lagoon blue two-button blazer, and loose matching slacks—paused to give the hackie a C-note, which explained how he got the guy to come here. The cab made its exit quickly, as if its driver knew being seen in these parts on a night like this would be embarrassing or maybe dangerous.

Young Colby strolled over, hands in his pockets, casual, a little smirky, the long, rather feminine eyelashes and product-dampened dark curly hair reminding me (as I'd observed the first time we met) of a Roman Emperor. I'd wondered if he was more Julius Caesar or Caligula.

Now I thought I knew the answer.

We didn't bother with a handshake.

"What's the joke?" he asked, hands on his hips now. He was smiling but irritation was in it.

"I didn't know there was one."

He gestured with contempt to his surroundings. "Why meet here, Mike? In the asshole of the city?"

"Privacy. Not exactly paparazzi around. Hey, can you think of any place more out of the way?"

He shrugged, smirking again. "Coney Island off-season. Which is now."

"I didn't think of that. You should've suggested it, when I called." My turn to shrug. "This'll have to do."

I went over and unlocked a door with a key I'd borrowed and gestured for him to step inside.

He did, and froze as he took in a room full of darkness but for a card table and two chairs in a circle of white courtesy of a spotlight beam from a klieg light high up.

He muttered, "What in the shit..."

I put a chummy hand on his shoulder. "They were shooting a movie here last week, and I visited. They haven't picked up some of the equipment yet. Thought this might be fun."

His sideways look included a curled upper lip over perfect teeth. "Fun?"

I gestured grandly. "I know how you like theatrics, Vincent. Melodrama. Well, that's disappointing. Thought you'd get a kick out of this place. More mood than anything the Tube offers up, that's for sure. Except for maybe the Dungeon Room."

He pointed to the table and chairs in the spotlight; they almost glowed in the otherwise stygian space. "What *is* this?"

"We're going to talk. Just the two of us. Unseen by anyone or anything, but for the ghosts of dead steers and butchered pigs and slaughtered lambs."

He started to bolt but I had him by the arm.

"No," I said, fingers tight on his sleeve. "You're staying. We have a lot to talk about. Your cab isn't waiting, remember? None out there to flag down, either."

"Hammer..."

"And you don't want me talking to anybody *else*, before you hear what I have to say...do you?"

"What the hell are you talking about?"

"Do I have to drag you?"

He shook his arm from my grasp. "No."

"Good. After you, then?"

He looked stricken, but then he swallowed, straightened and complied—whether from fear, curiosity or both, I couldn't say. At any rate, he strolled into the darkness, hands in his pockets again, heading toward the circle of light and the waiting table and two chairs. I followed close, but not too close. The last time I'd been in the dark with him, he'd tried to cave my little chest in.

The lighting gave us both an ivory cast, and the situation an unreal feel. Our chairs were opposite each other, as if I were about to tell his fortune.

Maybe I was.

I said, "I will make you a promise."

"Will you?"

"Let me put your mind at ease. I'm not greedy. I have no interest in any ongoing blackmail. You will pay me a flat fee, for services rendered. Considering your tax bracket, it'll be cheap at twice the cost. One hundred grand. You spend more on your yearly fitness club fee."

His chin came up. "You're right. I can afford it. But what I can't do is imagine what you could have to sell to me."

I tossed a hand. "Just your life."

His head went back an inch.

"Well," I said off-handedly, "there's no death penalty now. But your life of luxury, your exciting career of high finance, your clubbing and your latest conquest and your fun little hobby of killing people...which I think has been going on longer than

anyone might imagine, except perhaps the late Casey Shannon…
all that will be over."

"Will it."

"Yes. But they'll love you inside. Good-looking boy like you. My
advice is, partner up right away, with some big strong bruiser—
you don't want to get passed around. And you probably know
about soap and showers."

He thumped the tabletop with a forefinger. "If you have
something to sell me, Hammer, put it on the table."

"What I have isn't tangible. It's the results of my investigation
into your hit-and-run and the various killings that followed."

He huffed a laugh. "You can't use anything you may have
found. You work through an attorney, so you'd be violating the
client confidentiality privilege."

"Not at all. Oh, it'd be shaky ethically, I grant you…but *you're*
not my client, Vincent. Daddy is."

His blank expression was all the response I got, or needed.

"Your first line of defense," I said, "is not terribly impressive.
You have alibis for the killings of Kraft, Jordan, and Mazzini.
All performed over the span of a few days, by the way, and that
is impressive. But back to your alibis. Your father? Your current
squeeze? Weak, Vincent. Thin. Parents, wives, lovers, the most
worthless alibis in the book. Now, you may be rich enough,
successful enough, respectable enough, to make that play, just the
same. I mean, I'll bet your pater would hire one hell of an attorney.
Gerry Spence, maybe. How about F. Lee Bailey? Dershowitz
would be perfect!"

For the first time a frown had its way with that smooth skin.

"Why would *I* need a defense lawyer? I didn't do a damn thing."

I raised a gently lecturing forefinger. "What's interesting to me, Vincent, is that while you're clearly deranged, your victims are never random, as is so often the case with someone who gets off on murder the way you do. No, you always pick out someone...deserving. Someone who's done you dirty—like Sheila Ryan's abusive ex, for instance. Or like the prostitute who blackmailed you...oh, I know, I know, not established, but that *will* come out. And I'm guessing Roger Kraft tried to squeeze more money out of you, too, although you may just have been tying off a loose end. And Shannon—a decent man, but he hounded you unmercifully even after he was no longer a cop. Why should you have to put up with that? By the way, did he have anything? On that floppy disk you stole, I mean...and after all the trouble I went to in finding it!"

He stood. "That's enough of this bullshit. You don't have anything to say that even vaguely interests me. There's a coffee shop a few blocks from here. I'll call for a ride from there. Goodbye, Hammer. I'll tell my father to fire you first thing tomorrow."

I raised a "stop" palm and smiled. "Sit down and I'll tell you what *does* impress me. Not your pitiful line-up of alibis. No. I'm talking about your *Plan B*, Vinnie. You don't mind if I call you Vinnie, do you? It's a better name for a murderer than 'Vincent'—unless your last name is Price, maybe."

He thought about it. Then he smoothed his jacket—Armani again, I'd wager—and sat. "Plan B...?"

"Yeah. That's what the hit-and-run fakery was about. You *really* trained for that—getting into shape with a ten-degree black-belt *sensei*. Really going for it, learning techniques from an actual movie stunt man."

"I don't know any movie stunt man."

"Sure you do. Oh, I admit I don't have anything on those earlier kills—the secretary you undoubtedly raped and strangled, and the broker at your firm you ran down in that parking ramp. How many like them have happened over the years? Now, how you used the *hit-and-run* episode—that was cute."

"Cute?"

I corrected myself: "Ingenious. You devised a Plan B that covers every murder since you had your personality-twisting concussion. You played it to the hilt, the whole Jekyll and Hyde bit—plenty of witnesses to your uncontrollable outbursts to contrast with your otherwise normal behavior. I saw it myself, more than once. All the time you logged with doctors, who assigned meds, which I bet you didn't take, and constant psychiatrist visits… *that's* the Plan B—the groundwork for the insanity plea from the best lawyers Daddy's money can buy. Might take a year or two before convincing doctors you're well. Maybe you'd stage another accident with a blow to the head that 'cures' you. Clever. Sicker than hell, but clever."

Colby had started smiling halfway through my little speech. Then he stood and began to clap and laugh, the laughter sounding crazed to me, ringing off the brick walls.

He leaned toward me, hands on his thighs, his smile mocking. "I hear a bunch of theorizing, Hammer. I don't see a scrap of *evidence*. And I haven't confirmed a damn thing you've said, and why should I? You want a hundred k for *that*?"

"Well, I'll tell you one thing I don't want, and it's a hug. I know how that kind of hug can end up. Of course, the last time you tried it on me didn't work out for you. You got flipped on your ass." I gave him a nasty smile. "Here's a tip—don't wear a distinctive cologne to a killing. Detectives pick up on subtle little clues like that."

But for the tiniest curl of his upper lip, he was expressionless. "You have *nothing*."

"No, I have something." I was nodding. "I really do."

"Is that right?"

"Yes. You see, we aren't alone." I gestured behind me. "I have a friend in the darkness who's helping me. And making an audio recording of all this."

His single "Ha!" rang off the rafters from where the light was coming. "*What* do you have…besides your raving, your ranting, and your stupid suppositions? I haven't admitted to *anything*. And I'm not about to."

I got out the .45. "Sure of that?"

His smile disappeared but he remained calm. "Quite sure, Hammer. You waving your phallic symbol around to make up for your shortcomings does *not* impress me."

"Did you happen to read the papers yesterday? Catch the TV news, maybe?"

"What if I did?"

"It must have caught your attention. I'm referring to the coverage about your *other* accomplice—you remember, the one you haven't killed yet?"

He reddened. About time. "You are out of your fucking *mind*, Hammer."

"So some people say. Vinnie, I'm talking about Harry Strutt. Your stunt man instructor. You must have seen it—made page three of the *News*—four dead bodies in that farmhouse where Harry lives. I wonder who could have killed them?"

His eyes widened.

I went on: "They were a notorious bank robbery crew, you know. Some spirited citizen performed a public service, I'd say."

"Yeah. Yeah, you would."

"Funny, though—your buddy Strutt wasn't one of the victims. He must have got away."

"Good for him."

Another spotlight came down from above and its glow fell on a new member of our little cast. Maybe ten feet from us—bound into a chair, legs tied to the rungs, hands behind him, in a gray sweatshirt and sweat pants—was a familiar figure, easily identified despite the duct tape gag over his mouth and his bloodied, battered face.

"*Harry!*" Colby blurted.

I walked casually over, perhaps five feet from the newcomer. "You won't have to kill him, Vinnie. That wouldn't be deserving. You see, he was true to you. Loyal as the day is long. No matter what I tried, he refused to talk. He just would *not* sell you out. Still, he *is* a loose end and that's a problem. So I'll take care of it for you."

I fired at the bound man's chest—two shots whose echoing roars rang in the vast space, as the impact shook him in the chair, blood exploding out of him, two red flowering bursts in front but, in back, twin geysers carrying globs of bone and gore into the darkness, making little thumps and thuds and splishes on the floor, tiny things not at all commensurate with the big damage done.

Colby was on his feet, his arms and hands outstretched, as if there was something to be done, but there wasn't.

I fired once more, this time at the man's head, and a soupy slop of gray, red, and black splashed out his opposite temple, a small black hole appearing on the nearer one.

The bound figure slumped now, lifeless.

I grinned, nodded back at the slumped figure in the chair. "Your pal didn't think I'd do that."

I thumbed back the hammer on the .45—the click seemed to fill the big room—and walked back over to Colby.

"Of course, Harry Strutt was lucky," I said. "He went fast. You? You're going to get it nice and slow…arms, legs, then your belly, where it takes a good while, but don't worry, you won't pass out—you'll have plenty of time to think about what you did to a good man named Casey Shannon."

He was shaking now, like a bad dancer at the Tube. "You can *have* your damn money!"

I laughed. "No, Vinnie, that was just *theater*! Melodrama, my man! But it did get your *attention*, didn't it?"

"You bastard!"

"I get that a lot." I shoved the gun's snout into his belly. "Time to die, you psychotic son of a bitch…"

"No! *No!*"

My narrowed eyes looked into his wide ones. "Unless…"

"Unless what?"

I stepped back, the gun no longer in his belly. My voice was the essence of reason.

"Unless," I said, "you'd care to confess. With that on tape, I would have options. We could talk *real* money...regular payments..."

His eyes went wild, his so-white teeth bared. "I'll *confess*, goddamn you! I'll tell you everything!"

I stepped away and folded my arms, gun still in hand. "I'm listening. Sit your ass back down. And we're recording."

He spilled. Spilled everything, except for the two earlier murders. I let him have those. These four kills would be enough. And Jasmine Jordan *had* been blackmailing him, as I'd thought, foolish girl. Kraft had wanted more money, too. Foolish man.

"That's all," he said, exhausted.

"Lights!" I said.

The lights came up on the huge, mostly empty room, the bricks, the catwalks, the spots hung above, all came into sharp relief.

African-American hands, never really tied (they had controls to work), came around from behind the chair in which the "dead man" sat; then Thalmus Lockhart pulled the tight-fitting prosthetic mask off his head. He'd made the mask right there at the farmhouse, utilizing the corpse of Harry Strutt, who had split his skull when he fell, hitting that projection TV.

All it took was Vaseline, alginate, plaster tape, gypsum-base plaster, sulfur-free plasticine clay, gypsum slurry, and genius. And the bullet hits and squibs and gore effects had gone off perfectly.

To say that Thal and I were even now—for me getting him out of that barroom manslaughter beef—was an understatement.

Gotta love movie magic.

Colby was on his feet again, his eyes wide, his mouth making a sex-doll "Oh!"

Revealed also, now that darkness had been banished, was Velda at a table with a cassette tape set-up, and a big microphone pointed at us like a gun. Nearby was a borrowed NYPD video camera that Chris Peters was running—Chris was not here, if anybody asks you. A Homicide captain, say.

"You can go now," I told Vincent, returning the blanks-filled .45 to the shoulder holster. "You'll be hearing from the authorities. Now would be a good time to talk to your old man about countries without extradition agreements with the USA."

Any sane man would have run for the door and taken advantage of that generous offer. But, as we know by now, Vincent Colby wasn't sane and instead chose to lurch at me, and grab me by my head with both hands, like he was clutching a soccer ball to kick. As he tried to yank me down, to deliver one last crushing knee blow to the chest, my hands gripped his neck and I jerked and twisted. The result was the loudest *snap* anybody ever heard, its echo rivaling the .45 shots.

He collapsed into a fashionable Armani-clad pile of dead.

"No *sensei* taught me that," I told the corpse.

Velda was right there, hugging my arm. "Looks like he really *did* have a temper."

Chris called, "Mike—the camera was rolling. It got everything, including…uh, what you just did."

I shrugged. "Well, it makes backing up my self-defense plea this time a snap."

Velda didn't laugh at that—neither did Chris or Thal. Tough crowd.

But I took the opportunity to talk to the camera and offer an embarrassed smile.

"Sorry, Pat. I tried."

CHAPTER FOURTEEN

A white-haired butler in traditional black livery met me at the door to the co-op apartment. He was so ancient that he'd been doing this long enough for such a thing to be common among a certain class. That included the Colbys, of course, although frankly they may have been among the poorer folk housed in one of the twenty-two apartments on these sixteen floors. Billionaires looked down their noses at measly multi-millionaires in these here parts.

I was visiting, after all, an art deco, limestone-fronted monument to wealth on Fifth Avenue between 64th and 65th with a view on Central Park. Built between the wars, this was one of those white-glove palaces sporting a twenty-four-hour doorman at a canopied entrance and uniformed elevator operators waiting inside for those deemed worthy. I was expected, worthy or not, having called ahead. Otherwise, I couldn't have gotten in without a search warrant.

This was Tuesday and a laundered story of what happened in a certain Meatpacking District warehouse Sunday night had been all over the media on Monday. I'd met privately with my client's son to take a sort of deposition (so went this version of the "facts") about things I uncovered in my investigation of the chophouse hit-and-run; Vincent Colby became excited and attacked me—I defended myself with tragic results. For him. The personality change that followed his concussion was mentioned. Not much else.

Mostly it'd been photos in the papers of young Colby at the brokerage and out on the town, with footage on the tube of him at the Tube (and other clubs) as well as social and charity events. I spent much of Monday at One Police Plaza in Pat's office, viewing the video tape—Captain Chambers watching it with cold interest.

I won't go into how furious Pat was with me over my tactics, but he knew damn well having a non-police officer staging a charade like that had a positive side—namely, it made the tape's contents useable in court...or would have if Colby had lived to go to court. A citizen can't be accused of entrapment, after all. And for all his glowering, Captain Chambers had trouble holding back a smile when I looked at the camera and apologized to him.

For all his talk of putting Vinnie in stir to endure a lifetime away from privilege and freedom, Pat obviously didn't mind seeing the sick fuck dead. I knew I sure didn't.

But that attitude needed some sanding off at the edges for my client. I had a check in my wallet refunding his ten-grand retainer, though I doubted the old man would give a damn about getting his money back. I clearly hadn't delivered what he was after.

Vance Colby deserved the truth, though. Softened a little maybe, but when one day you have an heir ready to take over the reins of your successful brokerage, and the next you've got a dead murdering maniac for a son, nothing much can take out the sting.

And it would get worse. Soon Vincent Colby would be a notorious name in the headlines, joining the ranks of Bundy and Berkowitz, as more and more inevitably came out. With garish TV movies and documentaries to come.

What hit the papers this morning was the discovery of the body of Harry P. Strutt, dead of a blow to the back of the head, in the trunk of his Camaro, left on a country road outside Marlboro, New York.

After handing over my trenchcoat and hat, I was ushered through a black, white and gold deco-appointed foyer with a two-story ceiling and led past an ivory marble staircase with black and gold bannisters into a living room with, oddly, no *art moderne* touches at all.

This high-ceilinged, marble-floored living room with its golden-brown paneling and overstuffed furnishings—tall, burgundy-swagged windows looking out on Fifth—should have had a welcoming warmth. Despite the lived-in, overstuffed furnishings, a museum-like stuffiness pervaded.

Over a wood-burning, decorative fireplace loomed a large gold-framed portrait of a very beautiful dark-haired woman whose features prefigured her late son's; judging by the gown, I'd say the painting dated to the 1940s. For some reason I had a sense that when Vincent Colby's mother died (because this was surely her), she'd taken the warmth with her.

Of course, the fireplace wasn't lighted, so maybe that had something to do with it.

I was shown to the kind of bulging, tufted sofa you can get

lost in, along with the change in your pockets, gold-and-brown brocade and decades old. Plump brown leather chairs at left and right completed a sitting area on an oriental carpet, in front of the not-roaring fireplace with the painting supervising.

And then it hit me—nothing in here had changed since this lovely woman passed. I would give ten-to-one odds on that. This felt not so much like the chamber had been preserved, rather frozen in place, like her warm hovering expression. Either the artist was a liar or that expression conveyed genuine compassion, and a touch of sadness.

Had she died too young to pass her humanity on to her son? Or was he just born that way, blind and crippled to right and wrong?

A voice behind me wasn't what I expected.

"Mr. Hammer," a husky female voice intoned, "are you *sure* this is wise?"

I craned my neck and saw Sheila Ryan, in a black sweater dress that I guess was her idea of mourning weeds. She was walking briskly toward me, her red hair bouncing off her shoulders. She seemed cross. Well, I had killed her boy friend.

She planted herself a ways behind me, as I turned to look at her from the sofa. Her arms were folded on the impressive shelf of her bosom. Her make-up was subdued, but the red lipstick on her bruised Bardot mouth brought to mind blood. The green eyes flashed.

She got some indignation going. "Hasn't poor Mr. Colby suffered *enough*? What *more* would you put him through?"

I stood and moved around to her; we were rather small players in this orchestra pit with sitting areas, paintings worth thousands, and furniture that had been antiques decades ago, when the late lady of the house likely decorated it.

"Mr. Colby knows I'm coming," I said. "I spoke to him on the phone and he seemed calm enough. Or at least weathering this well, considering. I told him he had a right to face me, if he wished. He said he did. So here I am."

Her eyes bore into me. "It's ill-advised."

"Excuse me, Sheila, but…who are you to be handing out advice, anyway? And what the hell are you doing here? Why is it *your* place to comfort the father of a dead guy you'd been dating for, what? A few weeks?"

She unfolded her arms and, as they dropped to her sides, something winked at me…

…the rock on her ring finger.

I grabbed her hand, startling her, and had a good look at the diamond, which was ten karats anyway, in its simple four-prong setting. Your classic solitaire-style engagement ring. It said money, all right.

But there was a smaller band that spoke even louder.

I asked, "So you and Vincent tied the knot?"

"We did."

"When?"

The smile on her lips was barely there, but her eyes were laughing. Her cranky attitude had vanished. A cockiness was in its place.

"Saturday," she said. "City Hall. No one knew but the two of us."

"How romantic."

"We got the license Friday. Did you know it's just a twenty-four-hour wait in this state? I'm *here*, since you asked, to look after my grieving father-in-law."

I grinned, laughed. "So, then—congratulations are in order... Mrs. Colby. And of course condolences, since you're a widow."

Her chin came up and her smile was at once mocking and feral. "Maybe you'd like to kiss the bride."

"I'll pass. You know, since I killed the groom. But, hey—let's sit. Catch up a little." I gestured to the nearby sitting area by the fireplace.

"Why not?" she said and, her gait defiantly sexy, went over and settled her curvy self into the nearest brown leather chair. I sat on the sofa, close by.

She had an arm on either arm of the big chair, and put her feet up on the matching ottoman. Comfy. Cozy by the non-fire.

Her tone light now, the crossness wholly gone—it had been phony, anyway—she said, "I showed up at the door yesterday, in tears, and Vance welcomed me in and we wept together. He's such a sweet old boy. I'm moving in."

I stuck a smile onto my frowning face. "He's a little *old* for you, isn't he? And, anyway, you must already have a piece of all this— unless Vincent insisted you sign a pre-nup."

She shook her head and the red hair flew. "No pre-nup. Vincent was *nuts* about me, didn't you know? And it's going to be strictly platonic between me and the elder Colby. I'm the daughter he never had."

I nodded toward the choke-a-horse rock on her hand. "What did that bauble set your hubby back?"

She frown-smiled back at me. "That's the kind of question a person just *doesn't* ask."

"But I bet *you* did. How much?"

Proud of herself now, she said, "A hundred grand."

I had to smile. That was my bogus blackmail demand to her late husband.

I said, "How would you like to hear the real story of what went down Sunday night?"

"Sure."

I gave it to her—the whole megillah, from the charade at the warehouse and all the in's and out's of that, to how Vincent had confessed to the killings of Casey Shannon, Roger Kraft, Jasmine Jordan, and Gino Mazzini. And of course how he'd copped to the whole Plan B that the phony hit-and-run had put into play—the Jekyll and Hyde routine, after the faked concussion.

She frowned through some of that.

"It's awful," she said, "what you did to him."

"Yeah. I can be kind of a shit sometimes. Anyway, that's it. Well, there *are* a few things I left out."

She sat forward a little. "What did you leave out?"

I shifted on the sofa. "Funny running into you here. I had it in mind to look you up. Go over a few things. But the truth is, honey, I don't have a scrap of anything."

"A scrap of anything what?"

She was staring at me.

I stared back.

"Proof," I said, "that you were Vincent's accomplice in this, or anyway much of it. He had several accomplices, of course, but you I think were the key one. And that makes you an accessory to murder. At the least."

She wasn't looking at me now. "Does it really?"

I pointed at her and got her attention back. "I bet *you* were the one who threw off the light switch in that apartment building in Tudor City, when Chris Peters and I were looking for that floppy disk, with Vincent waiting in the hall to intercede. I'd love to have that disk, by the way, because it might clear up the last two murders—the girl your honey raped and strangled, and the broker he ran down in that parking ramp, God knows why. I wonder how long homicide had been his hobby? How many others there are?"

The red lips were tight now. "You're cruel."

"Is it cruel when a doctor delivers a diagnosis? And mine is that young Vincent was a sociopath or maybe a psychopath—the finer points of homicidal lunacy elude me. I was absent that day. But you, honey—you're no sociopath, or psycho, either."

"Gee, thanks."

"You? You're just plain greedy."

"Is that right."

I gave her the really nasty grin. "Your late husband was a lunatic who didn't realize he was one—and figured he could beat a murder rap by pretending to be what he actually was, then talk his way out, or fake another head-trauma injury, curing him this time. And in a year or two, he'd be graduated from the laughing academy. That itself was lunacy, of course, and you knew it—and sat on the sidelines urging him on, with dollar signs in your eyes."

She gestured to nothing in particular. "Why don't you try telling all this to old man Vance—see how *he* takes it. See if *he* buys it."

"He won't, huh? You think? Even though it's all true?"

"Even though it's all true."

I laughed softly. "I wonder if you were the one who came up with this whole crazy scheme—the hit-and-run farce outside where you worked…knocking off anybody who could cause the future Mr. and Mrs. Vincent Colby grief, like a blackmailing dominatrix and a boyfriend who battered you…*Gino* had it coming, did he? Maybe that's where it started. Getting back at a guy who liked to give his girl a black eye. Guess I'll never know, 'cause you sure as hell won't tell me."

Her chin came up again. "You're right. I won't. But I *will* tell you one thing."

"Please do."

She held up the hand with the huge rock glittering on it. "I was a waitress for a long damn time, Mike. I had acting dreams that went bust and the only one that came true at all was landing the hostess gig at that stupid chophouse. When I saw how much Vincent was into me…how the rich, so rich Vincent, had such a *thing* for me… how much he *wanted* me…how *obsessive* he was about having me…I said to myself, 'Sweetie, you finally caught a break.'"

"Sure," I said. "And it didn't matter that you'd originally thought of Vincent as a stalker. You knew once you married him, he'd self-destruct before too long. And if he didn't, well, you could always expose him as a murderer."

She was nodding. "I could, yes. And if he didn't get himself killed somehow, he'd be institutionalized. What *you* call 'Plan B.' Either way, I'd be set for life. The old man isn't going to live forever. Till then, I'll be on Easy Street. Until the whole damn fortune is mine."

How much he had heard I couldn't be sure—he might have been just outside the door. But I knew he'd stepped inside the room and heard her say, "Even though it's all true," and everything that followed.

Vance Colby didn't get my full attention until he was a few feet away and his hand came up and had the small gun in it, a little .22 S & W Escort; before that, he'd just been a distinguished mustached little man wearing sorrow like a coat of dripping gray paint.

She didn't see him.

What she saw was me easing my hand inside my coat—Vance's gun was pointing right at me, and if it coughed, I'd be coughing, too, coughing up blood. Then finally she heard his soft footfalls and whirled and stood, her hands out from her sides, fingers wide, as if looking for something to steady herself on.

"Mr. Colby?" she said. "Vance?"

He was pointing the gun at her now.

She ran to another door—there were plenty in that place—but she didn't make it. He caught her like a duck on the wing, in the back, the *crack* ringing in the high-ceilinged room, and she dove to the floor and slid on the slick wood, then shuddered and murmured self-pitying words before getting very still. Very quiet.

He looked at me. I was on my feet and the .45 was in my hand. I didn't want to do it and my expression told him so. But when—after a lingering look at his wife's portrait—he raised the gun, I knew I was not the target.

Sheila had been right.

The old man wasn't going to live forever.

TIP OF THE FEDORA

Although my intent is not exactly to create a historical mystery, I do attempt to place this novel (and others in this series) in the context of when Mickey Spillane wrote the material I worked from, and at what point in the Hammer canon this story appears.

To provide a background at least somewhat consistent with reality, I leaned upon Internet research. Among articles used for this purpose in *Masquerade for Murder* are: "Bellevue: The Best and Worst of America," Aaron Rothstein, *Public Discourse*; "Best Film Locations in NYC," *New York Film Academy*; "The Champagne City," Michael Shnayerson, *Vanity Fair/Hive*; "Five Fatal Punches," Sean Culver, *SCI Fighting*; "How to Make a Prosthetic Mask," Daniel Hayek, *Vimeo*; "Ivan Boesky and the End of the '80s Wall Street Boom," Peter Grant, *New York Daily News*; "'90s Anthem: So Many Gyms, So Little Time," Jennifer Steinhauser, *New York Times*; "NoHo's Cinderella Moment," Aileen Jacobson, *New York Times*; "One Street at a Time: Gansevoort Street," Michael Cunningham, *New York Times Magazine*; "Secret Karate 'Death Blow,'" *The Indulgent Samurai*; and the "Tunnel (Night Club)" entry at Wikiwand. Thanks to these writers and websites, and to others whose work I utilized in a more passing way.

My continuing thanks to Titan Books publisher Nick Landau, co-owner Vivian Cheung, and their editorial staff, in particular Andrew Sumner, who stepped up when he was needed; my gratitude to all of them for continuing to pursue the Mickey Spillane Legacy Project. The enthusiastic response to the Spillane Centenary-labelled publications in 2018 and '19, from the media and readers alike, was gratifying to those of us who consider the writer (he abhorred the term "author") a major figure in tough crime and mystery fiction.

Toward that end, Mrs. Mickey Spillane—Jane Spillane—continues to make these efforts possible. My wife, writer Barbara Collins, continues her stellar work as in-house editor, always tempering criticism with praise (you have been spared a phrase I wrote, and cut, after she wrote "Yikes!" in the margin).

Finally, my longtime friend and agent Dominick Abel continues to be indispensable where his clients Mickey and Max are concerned.

ABOUT THE AUTHORS

MICKEY SPILLANE and **MAX ALLAN COLLINS** collaborated on numerous projects, including twelve anthologies, three films, and the *Mike Danger* comic book series.

SPILLANE was the bestselling American mystery writer of the 20th century. He introduced Mike Hammer in *I, the Jury* (1947), which sold in the millions, as did the six tough mysteries that soon followed. His controversial PI has been the subject of a radio show, comic strip, and several television series, starring Darren McGavin in the 1950s and Stacy Keach in the '80s and '90s. Numerous gritty movies have been made from Spillane novels, notably director Robert Aldrich's seminal film noir, *Kiss Me Deadly* (1955), *The Girl Hunters* (1963), in which the writer played his own famous hero, and *I, the Jury* (1982), which set the template for a decade of violent-crime-based action blockbusters.

COLLINS has earned an unprecedented twenty-three Private Eye Writers of America "Shamus" nominations, winning for the novels *True Detective* (1983) and *Stolen Away* (1993) in his Nathan

Heller series, and in 2013 for "So Long, Chief," a Mike Hammer short story begun by Spillane and completed by Collins. His graphic novel *Road to Perdition* is the basis of the Academy Award-winning Tom Hanks/Sam Mendes film. As a filmmaker in the Midwest, he has had half a dozen feature screenplays produced, including *The Last Lullaby* (2008), based on his innovative Quarry novels, also the basis of *Quarry*, a Cinemax TV series. As "Barbara Allan," he and his wife Barbara's collaborative novels include the "Trash 'n' Treasures" mystery series (recently *Antiques Fire Sale*). The Grand Master "Edgar" Award, the highest honor bestowed by the Mystery Writers of America, was presented to Spillane in 1995 and Collins in 2017. Both Spillane (who died in 2006) and Collins also received the Private Eye Writers life achievement award, the Eye.

MIKE HAMMER NOVELS

In response to reader requests, I have assembled this chronology to indicate where the Hammer novels I've completed from Mickey Spillane's unfinished manuscripts and other materials fit into the canon. An asterisk indicates the collaborative works (thus far). J. Kingston Pierce of the fine website *The Rap Sheet* pointed out an inconsistency in this list (as it appeared with *Murder Never Knocks*) that I've corrected.

M.A.C.

*Killing Town**
I, the Jury
*Lady, Go Die!**
The Twisted Thing (published 1966, written 1949)
My Gun Is Quick
Vengeance Is Mine!
One Lonely Night
The Big Kill
Kiss Me, Deadly
*Kill Me, Darling**

The Girl Hunters
The Snake
*The Will to Kill**
*The Big Bang**
*Complex 90**
*Murder Never Knocks**
The Body Lovers
Survival…Zero!
*Kiss Her Goodbye**
The Killing Man
*Masquerade for Murder**
*Murder, My Love**
Black Alley
*King of the Weeds**
*The Goliath Bone**

THE WILL TO KILL

MICKEY SPILLANE & MAX ALLAN COLLINS

Taking a midnight stroll along the Hudson River, Mike Hammer gets more than he bargained for: a partial corpse on an ice floe. The body is that of an ex-police captain, who spent the last years of his life as a butler to a millionaire—also now deceased.

Were both master and servant murdered? Captain Pat Chambers thinks so. But to prove it Hammer must travel to upstate New York to investigate the dead man's family, all of whom have a motive for murder.

"Fans of the originals are likely to be satisfied."
Publishers Weekly

"Spillane has said that true heroes never die, and the same undoubtedly can be said of his greatest creation, Mike Hammer."
Criminal Element

MURDER NEVER KNOCKS

MICKEY SPILLANE & MAX ALLAN COLLINS

A failed attempt on his life by a contract killer gets Mike Hammer riled up. But it also lands him an unlikely job: security detail for a Hollywood producer having a party to honor his beautiful fiancée, a rising Broadway star. But it's no walk in the park, as Hammer finds violence following him and his beautiful P.I. partner Velda into the swankiest of crime scenes.

In the meantime, Hammer is trying to figure out who put the hitman on him. Is there a connection with the death of a newsstand operator who took a bullet meant for him? A shadowy figure looking for the kill of his life?

"This novel supplies the goods: hard-boiled ambience, cynicism, witty banter, and plenty of tough-guy action."

Booklist Review

"Max Allan Collins was an ideal choice to continue the bloody doings of Hammer."

The Washington Times

TITANBOOKS.COM

KING OF THE WEEDS

MICKEY SPILLANE & MAX ALLAN COLLINS

As his old friend Captain Pat Chambers of Homicide approaches retirement, Hammer finds himself up against a clever serial killer targeting only cops. A killer Chambers had put away many years ago is suddenly freed on new, apparently indisputable evidence, and Hammer wonders if, somehow, this seemingly placid, very odd old man might be engineering cop killings that all seem to be either accidental or by natural causes.

At the same time Hammer and Velda are dealing with the fallout—some of it mob, some of it federal government—over the 89-billion-dollar cache the detective is (rightly) suspected of finding not long ago…

"Collins' witty, hardboiled prose would make
Raymond Chandler proud."
Entertainment Weekly

"Another terrific Mike Hammer caper that moves non-stop like a flying cheetah across the reader's field of imagination."
Pulp Fiction Reviews

TITANBOOKS.COM

For more fantastic fiction, author events, competitions,
limited editions and more

VISIT OUR WEBSITE
titanbooks.com

LIKE US ON FACEBOOK
facebook.com/titanbooks

FOLLOW US ON TWITTER
@TitanBooks

EMAIL US
readerfeedback@titanemail.com

VISIT THE AUTHOR'S WEBSITE
maxallancollins.com